THE WILD DROVER'S
REVENGE

A
JACK RUTHERFORD
ADVENTURE

Published in paperback in 2019 by Sixth Element Publishing
on behalf of Ken Braithwaite

Sixth Element Publishing
Arthur Robinson House
13-14 The Green
Billingham TS23 1EU
Tel: 01642 360253
www.6epublishing.net

© Ken Braithwaite 2019

ISBN 978-1-912218-67-7

British Library Cataloguing in Publication Data. A catalogue record for this book is
available from the British Library.

Cover illustration by Vanessa Wells.

Printed in Great Britain.

THE WILD DROVER'S REVENGE

A JACK RUTHERFORD ADVENTURE

KEN BRAITHWAITE

Also by Ken Braithwaite

The Wild Drover
Available in eBook and paperback

Once again to Doreen and all our family who have been wonderfully supportive and encouraging.

Gillie Hatton and Graeme Wilkinson of Sixth Element continue their professional support.

John

with my best wishes.

Kevin B.

19 . 12 . 19 .

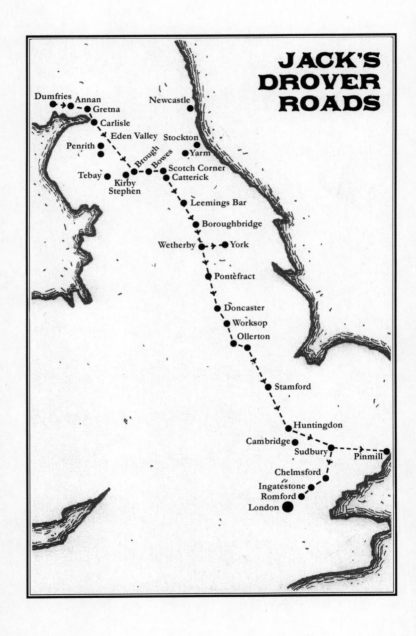

JACK'S
DROVER
ROADS

Dumfries • Annan
• Gretna
• Carlisle
Eden Valley • Stockton
Penrith • • Newcastle
Brough Bowes • Yarm
Tebay • • Scotch Corner
Kirby • Catterick
Stephen
• Leemings Bar
• Boroughbridge
Wetherby • • York
• Pontèfract
• Doncaster
• Worksop
• Ollerton
• Stamford
• Huntingdon
Cambridge •
• Sudbury • Pinmill
• Chelmsford
Ingatestone •
Romford •
London •

CONTENTS

CHAPTER 1
KNIFE TO THE THROAT

After a very early start I was looking forward to breakfast at home again. It was now June 1821, I had left home in late May and missed my wife and family. My son Giles was growing up fast and it was a real pleasure to be in his company. I had never appreciated what a wonderful sensation it was to have your son's small hand grasp your index finger in a tight grip. Giselle is a wonderful mother to the lad and we both now converse in French and English in front of him to encourage him to be bilingual. It has done me no harm either and provided some very funny moments.

Weary from the long ride back from Manchester and Liverpool and with quantities of tea legitimately purchased this time, I took the little used path behind Ridley House to look at some land adjacent to mine I had in mind to buy.

The land I was looking at comprised a farm house, outbuildings and 200 acres of very moderate pasture but with some potential. With proper care and some drainage I reckoned it could be made very profitable and I wondered just who I could trust with this task.

Under the tree lined path I only had glimpses of my big house as I surveyed the prospective land I hoped would soon be mine.

A growl from Dag, my damn great big wolfhound, and I paused to look in the direction he was pointing and saw a dust cloud from riders who quickly came ever closer to my front door. Three horsemen dismounted, one holding the reins of the animals and two running straight into my house, no pause, just rapid entry.

Calming Dag, I dismounted. We climbed over the nearby stone wall and, bidding the dog to keep quiet, we crept unseen to investigate what was happening.

Indoors I knew would be my wife Giselle, my baby son Giles, my father and mother, and Jeremiah and Hettie Ridley, the previous house owners. Probably my manager Albert would be present as well, enjoying a healthy breakfast.

Moving ever closer to the front door, I could see the ruffian holding the horses' reins had a hard look about him and carried a short sword in his belt, fortunately not in his hand because it was my intention to disarm him and lay him unconscious.

My name is Jack Rutherford, drover, farmer and now a substantial man after a successful land sale in Stockton-on-Tees last year. I stand 6ft tall and have had too many battles now to properly recall them, but all have been successful. The life of a drover is extremely harsh, living outdoors with your huge herd of cattle, sleeping rough and fighting off thieves, robbers, highwaymen and other nasty bastards, so much so that at 22 years of age I was a hardened practitioner in all forms of survival.

So without more ado I moved as close as I could to the waiting man and then sent my dog to distract him with a growl. Dag stands more than 3ft tall, is long, mean and a known killer, which is why we get on so well. Distracted, as I hoped, by the appearance of my dog, the man faced away from me and in moments I hit him with my handy cudgel, knocking him unconscious without a murmur.

Using his shirt clothing I ripped a makeshift strand to bind his hands and gagged him. I told Dag to stand guard, secured the horses very firmly, then crept quietly round to the back of my house where I entered the kitchen and removed my heavy boots. In stockinged feet and silent now, I moved to a small, little-used side door that gave in to the edge of the large dining room.

Pausing to peer through the crack in the door edge, my heart sank. Giselle, with her back to me and cradling our son in her lap, was sitting at the table and behind her a huge swarthy man held a knife to her throat demanding she sign a document on the table in front of her. All the rest of my family group and servants were sitting or cowering at the breakfast table under the gaze of another ruffian who held a pistol.

From my hidden position I viewed the scene with rising anger and concern; whilst I could easily half-kill the man with the knife before he knew what had hit him, the pistol-holding robber was a very different proposition.

Looking carefully at what was going on before me, I noticed that both my father, a former drover, and my new foreman, a former ostler, were in very close proximity to this man with the pistol, almost waiting for him to drop his guard to enable them to tackle him. In fact I was certain that was their intention but the knife at Giselle's throat and the baby in her lap made them extremely cautious.

Was there the chance then that if I could quickly overpower the knife wielding man, my two heroes would disarm the pistolier? It would be a huge gamble but I could not let this situation continue because in my thinking once Giselle had signed that document she would be killed instantly, as would my son and any other witnesses.

As always there was my long-handled dirk in my boot top, long experience had made that a habit.

Taking the dirk I leapt from hiding, flew at my wife's assailant and stabbed him fiercely in the top of his right shoulder. This was his knife arm and as I hoped, he staggered in shock away from her and fell, withdrawing the knife threat. My next action was to wound him again in the same arm and he dropped the knife, staring in shock at the blood pumping from his arm. Wild uncontrollable anger brought a savage blow to his exposed neck and he fell to the ground, very still.

In seconds my father and Albert had the pistol holding man on the floor after he glanced away in amazement at my dramatic appearance. They had a death hold on his neck until I coughed then they relaxed slightly and secured the man with his own belt.

My wife's attacker had been still for some time, so I kicked him in the ribs and heard the sound of bones breaking. He commenced writhing and continued this while I fastened him securely with his belt. Bleeding profusely he was making an awful mess on our floor and I determined to remove him quickly.

My mother, Jeremiah, Hettie and the servants looked on, shocked and aghast at my brutal treatment of these felons, forgetting just how close to death my wife had been.

I held Giselle close in my arms as she subsided into huge sobs and shook violently and after a lot of consolation she responded to a whimper from Giles, left my arms and comforted our son. Then all three of us surveyed the astounded gathering, who would have been aware of my reputation but of course this was the first time they had seen it demonstrated with some effect.

"Please all of you keep calm and help me to secure these two ruffians and the one outside. We'll give them a nasty shock for a while and then question them," I said.

Once matters had briefly settled down indoors, we carried the two principal ruffians outside and still secured, threw them in a deep horse trough face down. Their struggles to turn over thoroughly soaked their clothing and I left them to get completely cold.

At the front of the house Dag reluctantly moved from the very close proximity of my captive's neck and I hoisted the man to his feet. He had all the appearance of a former soldier with some traces of what was once a uniform but he stank horribly and was grimy and unshaven. With some belligerence he threatened me with extreme discomfort if I did not release him. Two very hard kicks to his stomach and he had difficulty speaking again for some moments. I think I established who was in charge.

Once he was able to speak again, I asked who had sent him but he refused to talk and firmly closed his lips.

He joined the others in the horse trough. It was getting a little crowded in there when I went indoors for a warm drink.

Lying on the table in the dining room was the piece of paper the villains wanted Giselle to sign and I examined it with some very considerable interest. I read its contents, albeit very slowly as the document was all in French.

After much study and help from Giselle, the most amazing statement appeared. The document alleged that Giselle's father had produced a bastard son, called Guillame Ribauld, who had laid claim to the whole of the estate of Giselle's murdered parents in line with French succession law.

Giselle was to acknowledge, in writing, his claim to the property, with her to receive nothing. This must have been as a direct result of my wife's letter to the Mayor of Saint Omer in France explaining she was still alive and wishing to know the whereabouts of her parents' grave and confirming her interest in the chemist's shop and any other property. This letter was written while I was on my first big drove for cattle in 1820 and before we were married. That first drove had given me the capital, with savings and smuggling money added, to start the second massive drove, and with those profits and my risky land speculation in Stockton-on-Tees, we had become very rich.

Now my understanding of the complex laws that Emperor Napoleon had introduced led me to believe, through my wife's comments, that all property of hers now vested in me as her husband.

Once Giselle and I were alone and that is always a problem despite the size of the place, we discussed the day's events. "My dear, do you imagine your late father could possibly have had an illegitimate son without you or your mother knowing?"

Giselle's response was most interesting. "Darling, I am an only child and there is a very good reason for that. My father suffered from what you in England call 'mumps', became very sick and poorly and was infertile from that time onwards. If as I believe, this man is younger than me, we can very safely assume he is an imposter."

I could hardly wander over to France and tell the Mayor that Mr Durrand was infertile but it made me realise that some prompt action was needed.

I detected an ominous pattern here. In 1819 Giselle was kidnapped to order and was brought to England to become a virgin bride to an English or Scottish Magistrate who had paid the notorious villain Silas Kirk to carry this out.

I believed I had killed Kirk when I pushed him under a moving coach and horses, but against the odds he must have survived and if he lived then I must assume he was the main link between Giselle's parents' death, at his hands, and this imposter.

To my very considerable alarm this was the only construction of events that would give rise to these villains' activities. Kirk knew that part of France very well and all the cut throats in the area.

My suspicion was that he had made use of this French imposter through his contacts abroad and that's how he was aware of Giselle's whereabouts. He it was who had murdered her parents and kidnapped my wife to be sold as a virgin bride to that magistrate and I was anxious to meet him and discuss the matter.

Not only had I rescued my wife from Kirk's clutches but he held a terrible grudge against me as a lot of his murderous friends had disappeared without trace after meeting me.

So, we now had three people on whom I needed to wreak vengeance. This French bastard, the magistrate who started the whole sorry mess and possibly Silas Kirk, if he was still alive.

I went outside where you could almost hear the chattering teeth as our prisoners wallowed in ice-cold water. Asked politely if they would like to tell me who had sent them they gave me the following worrying information having now become much more talkative.

They were former British Army soldiers, cashiered out

of the forces after robbing the dead on the field of battle and were former members of Sergeant Kirk's band of cutthroats. For £20.0s 0d each they were to hold Giselle until she signed the document then kill her and my son Giles and all witnesses and then leave once they had set the house ablaze.

Roughed up as only a drover and his crew could devise, they signed a document prepared by Jeremiah Ridley as a magistrate, and with broken arms and cracked ribs, all as they tried to escape of course, they were taken into custody in Brough to be locked up, their future to be very short, I suspected. Theirs was a hanging offence once proven.

CHAPTER 2
BORED AT HOME

Before the knife incident I mentioned earlier I had somewhat stagnated. Mine has always been a very active and adventurous life and I had achieved a considerable degree of success. The thrills of the open road and a herd of awkward cattle, bandits, thieves, rustlers, and cattle dealers all served to keep me alert, active and very involved daily. With my new found status as a fairly rich man I now found I missed the adventure and excitement. Even my daily practice with my sword seemed irrelevant but I stubbornly continued and it was excellent exercise.

After marrying my Giselle, we had been able to buy Ridley House from some dear friends, the Ridleys, and then move into this very nice building with its extensive grounds.

In my long absence in Suffolk in 1820, where I overwintered with my cattle, my wife had commandeered the knitted wool trade from all the drovers we accommodated in our lodgings and had established a very healthy trade in nearby Kirkby Stephen and elsewhere. She also used my supply of smuggled tea to start a series of 'Soirees' which attracted all the local gentry to try this latest fashion and parade every fortnight in their finery to Ridley House for tea and cakes. It made a lot of money and they were a feature now of the social scene.

At the time of my visit to Suffolk, Jeremiah and Henrietta Ridley, the former owners of Ridley House, had offered us accommodation in their huge premises when my father sold his own farm and building to try and retire.

Smuggled tea and tobacco had partly funded my cattle purchases but I was becoming concerned that my newfound status made me vulnerable to an enquiry by the Customs and Excise who had me on their watch list from times long past.

When we finally bought Ridley House from Jeremiah and Henrietta Ridley, we agreed that the massive house would easily accommodate them and asked if they would stay. They readily agreed and similarly, in my long absence and the increased 'trade' in tea soirees, my Mum and Dad, George and Mary Rutherford moved in so when I eventually came home there was a very full and active house awaiting me in which I took great pleasure.

Now I had money in the bank my social status had changed considerably and in many respects I felt vulnerable. My background could come back to haunt me and strange rumours came to me of a limping figure asking for my whereabouts.

My thoughts as I wandered about my land centred on three matters: Kirk's whereabouts and whether he had survived our encounter, the identity of the swine who had ordered Giselle's capture in the first place, then the possible repercussions from the ownership of property in France that would need a lot of managing for by all accounts, it was very substantial.

CHAPTER 3
SERVANTS

It was shortly after my return from my wanderings and settling down briefly to a rural life in Ridley House that Giselle raised the subject with me of servants. We were in front of the fire in the kitchen having just finished dinner when we got to talking together.

It was not a matter I had given any real thought to, being preoccupied with the house, its upkeep, mending all the outbuildings that had fallen into disrepair and creating a viable farm as well as looking after cattle kept on my land as part of a drove.

But servants, that gave me pause for thought and to question just what the costs would be and the benefits to us all.

Giselle was fully prepared for this discussion. It then occurred to me, she had given the whole subject much thought and gave me the facts as she saw them.

She said, "We are now the owners of a very substantial house with five principal rooms, six bedrooms, and five servants quarters in the attic of the building. This in addition to the hay shed, coach house, carriage house, granary, feed store, cow byre, drovers' accommodation, log store and a smelly privy that demand immediate attention from you and me."

I did not remind her that we also had a cellar that needed attention and a pump for our water that needed fixing but I had that in hand today.

I was given the clear message that everything needed tidying up, cleaning, whitewash on all the walls in the house and all the outbuildings, particularly the smelly drovers' rooms.

"When can you start on all these tasks?" was an opening remark that set me back on my feet and gave me a long moment of disquiet. She said, "If we had servants they would be given these tasks and enable us to concentrate on making a little more money. With my knitted items from the drovers and my successful Soirees I am making money but I am also seriously thinking of opening a ladies' dress shop in Kirkby Stephen. At all my Soirees the ladies ask me about the latest fashions from France and are fascinated by my accent and my clothes sense. I fully intend to take advantage of this by employing a seamstress in a shop I intend to open and I will charge very high prices for garments that I will be designing and making."

That certainly took the wind out of my sails. A dress shop selling high fashion in Westmoreland would be the last thing I could think of but we had the money now and my wife had an ambition that I would gladly encourage.

Back to servants… "Just what do you think we need, darling?" I asked.

Giselle said, "Certainly a housekeeper/cook, a kitchen maid and a chamber maid at the minimum and I have asked in the town about available help." Giselle further suggested that, "Your mother is getting too old to be dashing around at the pace she has adopted since she moved in and Hettie, God bless her, is no longer able to do the heavy work so it is falling on me to see to the running of this house. I don't expect you to see all these problems when you are so busy outside but we need to find a solution that we are comfortable with and can make work for us both."

The more we discussed the subject, the more I became aware just what a wonderful wife I had and how she gently brought me round to her way of thinking using logic and reason. Sitting together in that kitchen with Giles safely asleep upstairs, I counted myself a lucky man.

I wondered out loud, "When is the next hiring day for domestic servants, Giselle?"

She said, "According to Hettie and your Mother it will be June 24th Midsummer Day in Brough which is going to be in twenty-five days' time. I will attend with them. They both have a good idea of just the type of person we want."

Thinking things through with Giselle, I realised just how my status had changed recently and I was effectively now a Squire in the area because of my considerable estate.

There could be a problem. I would know the majority of the people who would be applying for posts. They would be aware of my background and I idly wondered if the junior staff would need to curtsy to me. That was a bridge I would cross in the fullness of time.

We continued talking together, lighting candles to enable us to continue sharing information. I kept putting extra logs on the fire and it was a thoroughly memorable evening.

So Midsummer Day saw us in Brough together, having used the carriage and horses so that Hetty and Mary could accompany us. It was very busy.

People milled about the Market Cross, moving from group to group, talking merrily and it had all the makings of a nice social occasion. My mother and Henrietta Ridley were well known in town as I was but I kept a very low profile on this occasion. Giselle was in charge, quite clearly, but consulted the other two ladies as they meandered through the gathered people all looking for a new employer.

On English Quarter days, hiring of staff is carried out. Suitable persons are questioned and references taken then begins the long haggle over wages, terms, days off and details of living accommodation provided. This ritual can seem endless but it has two distinct parts, employers seek reliable, trustworthy individuals who will 'fit in' to the household, hold prominent positions and in the case of the housekeeper be able to keep discipline and establish a rapport with her mistress. In this case it would be my wife Giselle but with the added complication of two very demanding ladies in my Mother and Henrietta Ridley.

From the intended new employees that we needed, first was to establish why they were available for employment. Had they recently been sacked? Had they shown a lack of ability? Did they have references to prove who their previous employers were? All very complicated.

Of course the other side of the coin was equally important. Future servants would be given accommodation in our house, be responsible for our meals, welfare, cleaning, emptying piss pots, ironing and washing, laying of table and sweeping and dusting. For this onerous task we would pay reasonable wages but they would expect to be told of their days off, if any, plus visits to home and deference to their new employer.

So you can imagine why I was keeping such a low profile here. Until a year ago I lived amongst these people as part of my parent's family and at the young age of twenty two it would be hard for local people to imagine the sudden change in my status, which would be difficult for them to come to terms with. Giselle was well aware of this dilemma and I knew she would choose her staff with this in mind.

Ever watchful, and with Dag at my side, I was tempted to slip in to the nearby tavern for a small beer when I was commandeered by my wife and the support team.

"We've seen two ladies who would be eminently suitable as housekeeper and we need your advice in which one to choose."

That was not expected and rather took me by surprise but I retorted, "Surely this is your area of knowledge, and hardly mine. I'm just a common drover and have spent so much time away I am unaware of your needs and wishes here. Tell you what, just point out the two ladies you have selected and I will wander round and have a look at them, if that will help? Stay here until I return but keep looking just in case." With Dag at my side I strolled around the edge of the throng and identified the two ladies selected and moved in their direction to get some impression of them. Housekeepers always stand very erect with an overbearing demeanour as far as I could see and they always clutch a large bag to their chests to glower over and certainly the first lady did just this. "I hope that dog of yours is properly secured, young man. I can't stand the sight or smell of the scruffy animals." This in a loud voice so people around would hear and take notice. I was taken aback by this comment and loudly suggested to the lady that, "Your frosty demeanour would put any dog in mind of bad meat and it would run a mile." That comment drew some smiles and I continued around the throng.

A hand came out to stroke Dag as I walked along and he stopped in his tracks, jerking me on his lead and proceeded to greet his new friend who ignored his size and stroked him and murmured something to him that set his tail wagging. This dog of mine is a killer and shows little regard for anybody but me and my immediate family so this was quite a novelty. Shortly I moved on, looking for that lady the girls had suggested but failed to find her and returned to them. "Can't find the second one but that first lady is a crosspatch and I want nothing to do with her. She doesn't like dogs."

Giselle smiled and said, "But you met the second lady. She was stroking Dag and talking to him, didn't you realise?"

I was immediately enthusiastic and the girls asked the lady to join us to enquire a little further in to her background. It appeared she had recently moved in to the area from Newcastle-upon-Tyne where her previous employer, a shipping merchant, had decided to sell his business and retire to Scotland. Although Mrs Blenkinsop, the lady we were speaking to, had been offered a position as housekeeper if she joined them, she felt more comfortable in Westmoreland and using her generous severance had moved in to rented premises in Brough. Her references were excellent, extolling her disciplinarian virtues with household staff and covered the wide range of skills she enjoyed. I noticed Giselle took particular note of her ability as a seamstress.

"Mrs Blenkinsop," said Giselle, "should we decide to employ you we need to discuss your wages, days off and holiday needs before we go any further." This they did right there and then. I kept out of it. Watching, I could see an understanding develop between Giselle and Mrs Blenkinsop. She deferred to Giselle's requests but made subtle suggestions that showed a keen understanding of our requirements. Dressmaking was included in this long conversation and at the end of it Giselle announced we had a new housekeeper whereupon we all shook hands.

Immediately Mrs Blenkinsop asked what other staff were to be employed and we mentioned a cook and a chambermaid. She stated that only two ladies in the throng would be worth considering in her opinion and if the decision was to be left with her she would point out the people she would select. Giselle agreed. A smiling lady joined us for a long talk and Mrs Dolly Denham joined us to be our cook and then after a further introduction and a polite curtsy young Becky Martin became our chambermaid.

Fully staffed and all in a good humour, the ladies embarked on our coach for the journey home and I walked with my new staff members, collected their minimal belongings which we put on a rented horse then we strolled up to Ridley House and chattered all the way. But it was immediately noticeable, as I hoped it would be, that I was deferred to by all three of them and quickly Mrs Blenkinsop established clearly who was in charge so a pecking order was agreed.

Once at Ridley House, Giselle conducted a tour of the place and allocated rooms to each, according to status, with Mrs B clearly impressed with the whole set up. Becky Martin could not believe her good fortune in having a small room entirely to herself, as she slept with four others normally and was in seventh heaven, she said.

From that moment on we had a smart, tidy, workmanlike and comfortable domestic arrangement and the looks of delight on the faces of all the busy staff when we held our first 'Tea Soiree' with which they assisted with was a sight to behold.

CHAPTER 4
POSSIBLE DROVE
FROM CARLISLE

Although I was bored with my enforced inactivity on the drove roads there was plenty to think about. In fact 200 acres of land adjacent to mine had come on the market recently, according to local comment. It would make a useful addition to my estate, so I was of a mind to investigate that a little further. With these thoughts rattling round my brain as I wandered about, I viewed with alarm a packhorse man approaching, six donkeys in tow and panniers on each containing the goods he hoped to sell.

Always I have kept in close touch with tinkers, packhorse men and itinerants. They shared the hedgerows and lanes with me on my droves and were a very useful source of information. But they all had 'sticky fingers' and nothing could be left in their vicinity that was moveable and valuable.

With this in mind I strode forward to prevent the cavalcade getting too close to my house when, as they neared, I recognised that most skilled of scallywags and thieving robbers, my almost good friend Reuben Connor whose miserable life I had once saved. It made no real difference, he would still rob me blind if he thought he could get away with it but we had battled hard just the once and he knew I had the measure of him.

Walking over to shake his hand, I greeted him jovially and against my instincts invited him in to the kitchen for a drink. Once he had secured his bad tempered donkeys, we wandered indoors where I asked for the kettle to be put on to make some tea. Reuben greeted the idea of tea with scorn and we eventually settled on a small beer for him and tea, my newfound beverage, for me.

We talked for a long time. He brought me up to date with all the goings on along the drove roads, I recounted my good fortune and new found wealth. Reuben stank, really smelled rotten, and I realised that Giselle's insistence on regular bathing had increased my awareness of the smelly conditions I had endured when I was on the road on a long drove. That could be the reason why we were left relatively undisturbed as we talked, as elsewhere the house bustled with all its usual activity.

Some very interesting information came from our long conversation and not all of it good.

Reuben had brought some smuggled tea for us but made it clear the Customs were on to him and me and it was time for me to establish a more regular form of supply using reputable agents.

He suggested I considered travelling to Liverpool where many reputable merchants had their premises and he would give me the names of two good agents who could deliver regular packages. I suspected I was talking to the regular delivery man but left that aside.

He then mentioned that on his way back from Liverpool, he had visited Manchester and in particular the cattle market which was devoid of beasts. Manchester had grown far bigger with the advent of steam engines and they powered some cotton mills that employed a huge work force all of whom needed feeding and meat was a popular but expensive choice.

In other words there was a demand for cattle and as this was March, not a lot of beasts were coming to be bought. Prices were high and likely to go higher. This had my undivided attention straight away and it was further sharpened with Reuben's next remark.

Carlisle had seen a big increase in cattle this early spring. Mild weather had brought many Irish beasts across the water to Whitehaven where they were heading down the edge of the Solway Firth before making for the Midlands and London Markets to arrive in late spring. This mild spell had encouraged many Scots herds as well and in his opinion good trade could be had in Carlisle if I was quick.

Then the bad news. I was correct in my suspicions, Silas Kirk had survived the incident with my horse and carriage, he was alive and well. His femur had been broken in the accident, badly re-set and he walked with a very distinct limp. He had sworn to kill me at the first opportunity, so once again my back was exposed to a lurking danger.

Reuben's next news jolted me further. His enquiries,

at my instigation, revealed that the slimy bastard who had ordered the kidnap of my wife was none other than a Cedric P. Cleasby, recently moved from Scotland to Cumberland and appointed a magistrate in the area.

According to Reuben, rumour had it he deflowered maidens on a regular basis, having paid for them to be forcibly removed from abroad, claiming they were 'married' to him when they complained of harsh mistreatment. His preference was for young ladies from France who were either orphaned or had one parent, the intention being to kill any parent, leaving the maiden bereft of kin and taken to a strange land.

A real nasty piece of work and now protected from prosecution by his being a magistrate. This was the beast who had 'ordered' my Giselle from Silas Kirk, only my intervention preventing her falling in to his clutches.

Then some more interesting news. This Cleasby, rich beyond belief through family mill ownership, had professed a vast knowledge of cattle and was in the market to purchase specimen bulls to be offered for stud to discerning farmers. That could be interesting as I was determined he would meet a very nasty end.

I paid Reuben for his smuggled tea, took details of his contacts in Liverpool, paid him a handsome fee for 'information' and cleared him out of the house before he could pinch anything. Then opened all the windows!

CHAPTER 5
DISMISSAL OF ALBERT ATKINS

One thing puzzled me, my new foreman Albert Atkins had been appointed by me in Stockton and I had purchased a horse and carriage to bring him and his wife and two children over to Brough to live nearby and act as my Farm Manager.

My carriage and a fine horse arrived safely but I could find no evidence that Albert's wife and children had accompanied him. Very strange.

I spoke to Giselle about this strange happening and she confirmed that local rumour had it that Albert was living alone and drinking heavily with an unsavoury crowd in Brough. Indeed she had twice reminded him of his duties whilst I was away and he had adopted a very surly attitude to her which caused her to be extremely firm and remind him he was an employee.

Thinking on these remarks I strolled outside and examined the crops I had instructed him to plant some time in the early Spring, namely, swedes or turnips which I knew from experience would provide valuable Winter feed for any cattle we had remaining after the September sales. That, and the fields I had set aside for hay making and barley, should give us ample supplies for the cattle and horses we keep.

My swedes were planted but looked to be very thinly sown; weeds had already established themselves for lack of proper hoeing. I knew I had paid Albert to employ village men to carry out that task and I was now getting very cross although I realised that in my moping about 'bored' I should have taken a lot more notice of the activity on the farm.

Next, the hay field. It was now late June and a team of men should have been working the field with their scythes cutting the meadow grass and allowing it to dry but there was no activity and it was almost too late.

My field of barley was growing but again very thinly spread from a haphazard sowing and I resolved to sort this out immediately, so heading for the house I asked Giselle to spare me a few moments so we could discuss matters. More and more I find Giselle way ahead of me in her thinking and actions. She too had noticed the failures I had now uncovered, had remonstrated with Albert who was asked in no uncertain terms to hire men immediately in town, bring them back and start weeding and haymaking.

Perhaps unwisely, she had given him a small amount of money to pay a starting wage and encourage interested men to start quickly.

That was at 9am this morning, but it was now midday

and no sign of him. I saddled a horse and rode quickly the mile or so to Brough where I started by visiting the many taverns which I knew very well. Finally I found him in the George and Dragon, absolutely inebriated and shouting and yelling about work for all but he needed paying in beer. That was as much as I heard as I quietly entered having first removed my coat and hat and loosened my long dagger in the side of my boot.

Sitting in the corner and listening further, it became apparent that he was very well known here, drank copiously and demanded money up front from those who wished to work at Ridley Hall.

Finishing my small beer, I stood, walked over and tapped Albert on the shoulder, then stood back and sure enough a knife appeared in his hand that would have disembowelled me had it connected, but he missed, overbalanced and I hit him with a huge blow to the back of his neck and he fell to the floor where I put my foot on him to hold him in place. He's a very wiry little bugger is Albert and I took no chances, found string in my pocket and tied him securely, all in a moment.

A profound hush had fallen in the tavern. My reputation for hard action was known so I made for the bar, ordered a further small beer and asked if any of those present would like to work for me, haymaking or weeding turnips. Of the twenty men in the room ten volunteered and finishing my ale I asked them to be at Ridley House in two hours, sober and with their chosen tools.

I paid the landlord to make sure Albert had suffered no

great damage and asked him to get the scoundrel to come to see me next morning to discuss his fate, then I left.

By 3pm that day, four men were weeding the swedes and turnips, under my instructions at first, then the rest started mowing the long grass and worked very well indeed. They left at 7pm with a half day's wages and were anxious to come back the very next day at 8am and put in a full day's work which I agreed with.

Explaining my actions to my wife later on, she agreed that we would get rid of Albert, who she understood, had left his wife and children in Stockton where she heard she had found a new replacement for her husband, a man who did not beat her and the children and worked regularly for a decent wage.

Giselle then stated she would manage the temporary employees for me and I agreed that would be an interesting way forward.

CHAPTER 6
BLACK BULL IN CARLISLE

Boredom behind me, I was on my horse that same day, having kissed Giselle and baby Giles and being wished a safe journey by my Mum, Dad, Jeremiah and Hetty, leaving a crestfallen Albert to collect his belongings and tools. Albert Atkins and I had shared an adventure or two on the road to Dumfries and back after I needed a good man with horses to get me across country quickly. He had proved his worth then and also in a fight we had against ruffians and I had appointed him as my Manager to control my burgeoning estate. But this recent episode had saddened me. I little realised how addicted he was to drink and we parted with me giving him his wages to date but no reference which he swore was his entitlement and he would have his revenge on me. I placed him under no delusions as to what would happen if he caused me grief and we parted on less than friendly terms.

Grabbing a horse and taking a spare animal with me, I shouted for my Dag and we set off at a brisk pace for Carlisle.

Three long days later and carrying a lot of money with

me, I reached my destination and made for The Sands area where cattle gathered and sales took place. It takes time to look around at what's available. Some cattle thrive on better pasture by the trackside as they travel, others thin out very quickly if they have been moved at a pace and all this needs to be taken in to account. With no Top Man with me, I hoped to engage a suitable drover as I was too young to be considered for the position. Only married men over thirty could be considered but I had a good knowledge of the trade and knew just the kind of man I needed.

Over the next two days I surveyed cattle arriving and leaving and at night I wandered into well known taverns to catch the gossip and identify my possible herdsmen. All the usual idiots were in evidence plus some wise old heads and those I spoke to at length, finding that there was one man, John Fisher who, if available, would join me and safely deliver my herd but at a price. He would, I gathered, supply men and dogs.

During these conversations I had watched two big scruffy blokes checking my movements and as I moved from tavern to tavern they dogged my footsteps. Unknown to them that wolfhound of mine was dogging their steps, but very quietly, so when they attacked me in an alley near the town centre it was a short hard battle. One man with a knife was disabled smoothly, his wrist broken and his ribs caved in. His comrade was just saved from a horrible death when I stopped Dag from tearing his throat out, but blood was pouring from his wound and I had to tear his shirt and make a bandage to stem the liquid. Both were dazed by the ferocity of our attack and the terrible punishment meted out. I left them sobbing in the gutter, one trying to stem the blood from his mate's throat. My money remained safe but for how long?

Next morning I tracked down John Fisher and we had a long discussion. He had a big farm on the outskirts of Carlisle and if I employed him and his men and dogs then I could overnight my cattle on his premises before we set off for Manchester which was not a market he had ever visited or contemplated. My reputation as a drover was known to him and we got on well. In fact he mentioned that a particularly good herd of one hundred and fifty cattle was approaching The Sands and we should think about examining them, although he had heard there may be a problem.

Without more ado we reached The Sands and within the hour the big herd appeared and with it the biggest meanest bull I had ever seen. The ring on its nose showed bleeding and it was prancing about and causing its three handlers some serious problems.

Wandering round these cattle it became obvious that they were in excellent condition so I approached the owner/drover and commenced negotiations. Nobody else came anywhere near whilst I spoke which raised my suspicions that there was something wrong. I looked to John Fisher for advice but he just shrugged his shoulders and put his hands in his pockets, not much help there.

Then it became apparent, this herd would only be

sold if I purchased the crazy bull as well. Looking at the animal I realised it had a very vicious, wild temperament and was practically uncontrollable but at the same time it was of a wonderful proportion, well muscled back legs, a straight back and huge bollocks. At the back of my mind I recalled Reuben's comments about this Cleasby man and I wondered if this bull could be his nemesis.

Price-wise the man wanted £10.0s.0p for his beasts and would include this crazy bull at the same figure but I had to take them all. If rumours, on which I lived, were correct, I could get about £12.0s.0p or more in Manchester but that bloody bull; a problem perhaps, unless I could separate the damn thing, put it somewhere safe and come back to it later in the year. The germ of an idea was developing involving Mr Cleasby the so-called cattle expert.

I offered cash on the nail out of my satchel to the seller and his eyes bulged a little to see the pound notes, just as I hoped. Normally drovers negotiate a price, then pay a percentage down, say a tenth in cash and the balance in two or three months hence. But this is very dependent on the reputation of the drover and is a big gamble for the seller and buyer.

Craftily I had brought a big stash of pound notes with me which had attracted the villains the night before but now stood me in good stead and by flicking some notes about I brought the price down to £9.10s.0p per beast. We settled up at that, on the spot, me getting a formal invoice for the cattle I had bought.

CHAPTER 7
MANCHESTER
CATTLE MARKET

Smiling, I put my arms on John Fisher's shoulders and mentioned that we had a deal which I'm sure he would enjoy. I explained his terms of employment which he accepted somewhat reluctantly being a hard businessman. Then I dropped my bombshell.

For a suitable fee I would entrust him with my crazy bull to be kept at his farm, at my expense.

Fed, watered, kept clean and exercised regularly, as an added bonus he could cover up to twenty cows with the big randy beast without any extra cost to him. Taking the wind out of people's sails is a well-known expression and amply demonstrated at that moment. He spluttered and swore and cursed and stamped his feet and all the usual performance, then grinned and we agreed a price.

Two days later saw us on the track to Manchester, a distance of one hundred and twenty miles which we covered in fifteen days. It was a difficult journey made reasonable by the weather being mild, and John Fisher's men certainly knew the droving trade. We made good time, stopping two days each week to rest the cattle and ourselves. It was hot dusty work as always.

Eventually we arrived at the almost deserted Cattle Market and during the next day a flood of buyers surged round my beasts and prices rose and rose.

In the end I sold the whole herd in small parcels to local butchers and obtained an almost unheard of price of £12.10s.0p, a profit of £3.0s.0p per beast, making me £450.0s.0p.

Even after I had paid John Fisher and his men and all my toll costs and overnight stops, I still had £410.0s.0p. Not bad.

Hiring a horse and making sure Dag was with me, I then travelled the road to Liverpool to meet some tea merchants. Without the distraction of cattle and keeping a wary eye open for highwaymen, we covered that well trodden trail at a steady pace, dusty but content.

Reuben had suggested two companies I might approach to do business with and I was looking forward to the discussions. Leaf tea is sold in packets containing a pound of tea. Normally on the outside of the package it states '1lb' and costs 3s 8d in reputable grocer's shops. I needed to buy enough tea to provide cups to each of thirty people once every two weeks, because that's just what the ladies had achieved with their Soirees.

Now by my reckoning at a Soiree, thirty plus people would attend and drink two to three cups each so I needed about half a pound of tea per session with two sessions a month over three months, about 3lb of tea.

All this thinking on horseback was very wearing and I was glad to see Liverpool appear in the smoky distance. I booked in a reasonable tavern, fed Dag, enjoyed a good meal and woke early after an excellent night's sleep. Ostlers had fed and stabled my hired horse. At my request he was brought round and I mounted and rode away, dog at heel.

CHAPTER 8
LIVERPOOL TO BUY TEA

Despite my new wealth, I remain at heart a cattle drover and wore a drover's hat, woollen shirt, loose top coat, breeches, leather gaiters and heavy boots. In other words a scruffy looking bloke, not to be messed with and that served me well. The streets of Liverpool were rough. The city stank to high heaven from sewage left in the streets and was filled with ragged urchins, downtrodden people and the look of thieves about each corner. I was very wary.

From the address Reuben gave me I made my way to a very busy but grimy street of warehouses and offices and found the premises of Hedley and Watson, Grocers, Wine and Tea Merchants. I secured my rented horse, bade my dog to "sit" and went to the door of the shop.

On entering I was impressed at the total silence in the dark interior. How they ever found a customer puzzled me, but a door opened and a large florid officious-looking brute of a man came bounding over to me in an aggressive manner.

"You scruffy miserable piece of dirt and filth, get out

37

of this shop immediately or I will give you the hiding of your life."

Now that's a very interesting way to greet customers but on reflection, I did look a little down at heel, but not, I thought, enough to warrant that sort of behaviour so I teased him.

"You must be feeling very powerful and strong working with girls all day and no man to challenge you," I mentioned as I dodged his outspread arms and moved swiftly away. "How would you feel if I took you outside and made you regret every word you have said?"

That had the desired effect, two more rapid advances on me but I was young, agile and bloody cross. Once we had danced round the shop floor a few times, he started to pant and that's when I opened the door, stood outside and challenged him to "get me" and the silly sod fell for it.

Once outdoors he shouted obscenities and rushed at me but this time I stood my ground and hit him hard in the stomach, then his ribs, then his face and finally kicked him on his knackers with a good hard kick. He went down screaming and caught his ear on a protruding stone. Blood poured to the ground from his wound in a dramatic way.

I was all for leaving him but as fortune would have it, the door to a nearby shop opened and a lady appeared. She was about to give the villain assistance, but I stepped in and raised the ruffian from the ground and looked for support. None came, people stood back in awe but no one came to help except the first lady. She said, "Bring him in to my shop now. I have some bandages and a sponge to clean him down. He is a really horrible bully but still a human being."

Before I could dispute this, she had me carry this big youth into her shop where she laid him on the shop floor, demanded water and cloths from her staff and spent the next ten minutes bringing the big sod back to semi-normality.

To my astonishment, as I sat back and watched proceedings, it appeared I was in another tea selling shop so I kept very quiet and watched.

My assailant sat up, glowered at me and attempted to rise but fell back weakly and was offered a cup of water and told to stay still. The lady who came to the rescue then turned to me and with some asperity said, "And who do you think you are, young man?"

Somewhat taken aback at this interrogatory approach, I said that I was Mr Jack Rutherford of Ridley House, Brough in Westmoreland and I merely went across the road to buy some tea.

That stopped things in their tracks. "Who did you say you were?"

I repeated myself.

"But you look like a scruffy drover," she said, slightly mollified and I retorted that that is what I was until I made a successful cattle sale and land investment.

"Do you own Ridley House then?"

I agreed that indeed I did.

She went very quiet. The idiot on the floor gaped and looked suitably embarrassed.

Mrs Clark, for this was the lady who I was addressing, was the principal partner in Clark and Dowkes, tea merchants and many other things based here in Liverpool. We kept talking. Word had spread about the successful Tea Soirees in Brough and they, as tea merchants were anxious to know if they could quote to replace my present suppliers. That was a laugh but I decided to come clean.

Of course Mrs Clark knew of Reuben Connor and his smuggling activities and she was suitably cross with me for not having made her acquaintance earlier but understood my need for instant cash to buy cattle and prosper.

Having escorted the idiot from over the road back to his shop, we repaired to her office and I took an immediate liking to the lady. She was very business-like, gave me a card with her name and address on it, and suggested we could explore the possibility of her becoming my supplier.

That put me in a bind but I asked if she ever used Reuben Connor for her deliveries and she went very quiet for a few moments then gave a wry grin. "I realise now that's how you are able to provide your tea. But whilst we are in business together everything will be conducted properly and with full accounts and invoices." She gave a knowing wink and said, "But I'm sure Reuben Connor will act as your delivery man."

After some discussion she agreed that I would deposit £1.0s.0d with her and purchase immediately 3lb of Connoisseurs Tea at a discounted price of 3s 6d per pound. First delivery I would take with me but subsequent deliveries every three months would be made by Reuben Connor who would bring back the money for her. This way she would always be a little ahead in payment. She and I gladly agreed and shook hands on the deal.

Pleased with my purchase and the long term arrangements I had made, my horse, dog and I turned thankfully from Liverpool and commenced the journey home to Brough, blissfully unaware of the coming battles.

Once home I would make my plans to buy the additional land I had previously considered.

CHAPTER 9
RETURN HOME

Having dealt with Albert Atkins and the knife incident that I mentioned previously, life settled down again and a smooth running household gave me great pleasure and enjoyment.

Giselle and I were able to have some long discussions about matters in France. I was aware of the chemist's shop in Saint Omer that her parents ran before they were murdered by Silas Kirk but it now transpired that the family also owned a considerable acreage of pasture in the surrounding area.

Giselle mentioned, "When I wrote to the Mayor in Saint Omer all that time ago, we were not married and I have a nasty suspicion that the letter was waylaid in the Mayor's office, which was always a hotbed of rumour and dispute. It was the least organised official department I have ever heard of. In fact it took my father many months to obtain the renewal of his licence to be a chemist and I suspect he fell out with the Mayor when he went to complain about the delay."

This painted a very gloomy picture of officialdom in France taking advantage of Giselle's parents' demise.

By Giselle writing to the Mayor, the authorities in France were aware of her continued existence and would wish to transfer the ownership of all the property to her. But of course, as we were now married it appeared that all the property now vested in me as her husband under the new Napoleonic Code that had been established in 1810 or thereabouts.

Over many hours of discussion round the fireside after work and with all the family and friends gathered together, we came to the conclusion that Giselle's letter to the Mayor had been intercepted and read by some unscrupulous rascal and a plot made to disinherit her from what appeared to me to be a considerable estate.

Giselle had no other family or kin in the Saint Omer area of France which rather threw us as to the problem of the future management of the properties so I made the decision to travel over there by any means possible, assess the situation, deal with any issues and resolve a future plan of action once on the scene.

The sudden attack at my home made me very aware of how vulnerable we were in this remote part of Westmoreland and I gave some long hard thought to the security of my now extended family should I decide to risk the journey to France.

Worrying about this, plus the possibility of further land I wished to acquire brought me to a state of despair but I did not want to place any additional burdens on all my kin and friends. I spent many days considering how best to secure my family and property in my absence.

CHAPTER 10
JOSIAH AND
MARGARET LIDDELL

Alone in the kitchen I made a cup of tea in my battered old tin mug and then went outdoors onto the estate into the spring sunshine to cut some more logs for the many fires the ladies kept burning in the house. Followed everywhere by my damn great big wolfhound, it was a delight to be outdoors again, viewing progress on my farm.

My wife, Giselle, son Giles, my parents and Jeremiah and Henrietta Ridley had taken the horse and carriage and headed for Brough to 'go shopping' although as this was a Friday the chances are there would be more available than on a normal day. The market would be in full swing which was doubtless the reason for the happy crowd that left in such high spirits.

Long steady blows with my axe split the logs to my entire satisfaction and it was a delight to be working hard and enjoying the warm sunshine. There are things to ponder when you have a simple manual task to perform, and the work and the looming visit to France kept my mind fully occupied.

Steadily the pile of logs increased and after half an hour of steady effort I grabbed my almost cold tea and stood to take a drink.

My eye was caught by four people trudging up my long drive carrying what appeared to be all their worldly possessions on their backs. Strange, I knew of no expected visitors and watched their slow progress with some concern.

I went in to the kitchen, put a log or two on the big range fire and filled the large kettle in the absence of immediate staff. Those people who were approaching would need a cup of tea and goodness knows we had enough tea in the house to keep an army going.

Outdoors again the small family group, that I now perceived it be, came ever closer until they were upon me, standing respectfully a distance apart. Droving is a rough trade and I meet many bedraggled people in countless numbers on the roads, but this was such a truly downtrodden, weary, frightened and wretched group that my heart went out to them.

Peering hard at the large gaunt male, I tried to make out his features behind a scruffy beard. His wife clung to his hand, but the two skinny youths stood off in a guarded way and watched me like hawks, extremely protective of their parents and I liked that.

As I was about to speak, the father made himself known to me. "Mr Rutherford, some time ago you bought some cattle from my farm in the Eden Valley and your Letter of Credit saved my family and I from a very harsh, hungry winter. I wonder if you remember me?"

It all came back. I'd bought the cattle on a whim to give these folk a chance to survive, the cattle had been in good condition but a little thin when I got them but good pasture brought them to tip top condition and I sold them for a profit. This was a good farmer.

"Forgive my poor memory please and remind me of your name," I remarked, at which he removed his hat and introduced himself as Josiah Liddell.

"Right, Josiah, the kettle's on and I would like you to join me in the kitchen for a cup of tea."

He demurred. "Mr Rutherford, I am here looking for work and you are the only person I could think of to approach. Two weeks ago all my cattle and two sheep were rustled away, the new landlord came and doubled the rent and has now thrown us out with whatever we could carry. I have left an old pony and cart in Brough with a few other things we have salvaged. I am desperate."

"Mr and Mrs Liddell and family, I cordially invite you to come in to my kitchen, enjoy some tea and a little refreshment because you may be the very solution to my problems. But before we go in, could you please introduce me to your family as the last time we met these two young men were leaning on a wooden farm gate and listening to our conversation very carefully."

"Mr Rutherford, may I introduce my wife Margaret and my sons, James and Theodore known as Teddy."

We all shook hands. As we moved to the kitchen I said, "It's Jack to you from now on, Josiah, and I wonder if you prefer that or Josh," at which he smiled hugely and said, "Josh will be fine, Jack."

Margaret agreed I could used her first name to our joint delight but I looked at the youngsters and suggested Mr Rutherford would be fine rather than Sir.

When we sat at the kitchen table, I realised these folk would be desperately hungry but would not appreciate any charity so I had an idea.

"James and Teddy, if you could look in the pantry you'll find some big loaves of bread, some butter and some lovely jam. Can you slice some bread, butter it and spread it with jam and bring it out on a plate while I talk to your Mum and Dad."

They were off like a shot, giggling and laughing which was a joy to see and hear and I turned to Josh and Margaret.

"We dealt successfully last time we met. You certainly know your cattle and I have been mulling over a further expansion of the farm." I went on to explain my good fortune in a venture and I was now the owner of Ridley Hall and its present acreage which we used to accommodate drovers and allowed cattle to graze the pasture as they passed through on a drove.

Suddenly a huge plate of jam sandwiches appeared and some very hungry people lashed into the plate with alarming verve, all laughing and relaxed. I hoped this was not too premature but it seemed a good start.

Once replete and after numerous cups of tea I put my ideas forward.

"Yes, I would like to employ you, Josh, and I could

provide very basic accommodation for you all but it would need hard work to be made properly habitable."

That statement brought gasps of delight and Margaret broke into tears. I'm sure if I'd looked I might have seen a tear in Josh's eye but I avoided direct contact and busied myself collecting cups and plates.

At my suggestion we all went outside into the fresh air where tears were surreptitiously wiped away with skirt edges.

Accommodation for drovers is always well removed from the main buildings because, frankly, they stink. Our drovers' lodgings were nearby and comprised one half of an old building that I had repaired and improved. One side was their lodgings and very, very basic. The other half of the building comprised three downstairs rooms and three bedrooms on the upper floor with a small room for a with a wash stand. The drovers' portion was at present empty.

I asked the family to accompany me to the poor half of the building and suggested they could use that as their home temporarily and whilst Josh remained in my employment. We had not discussed any terms, nor was I about too until I laid my second plan before him.

Margaret, Josh and the youngsters stared aghast at the accumulated rubbish piled in the building and then slowly and carefully examined each room from top to bottom, just as I would have done, but they made only passing comments quietly to each other as they passed from room to room.

Outside again I asked Margaret what she made of it all. There was a very long pause, then a slow smile and, "Do you know, Jack Rutherford, I think I could make that a temporary home if you will have us."

That was what I wanted to hear. "Margaret, have another good look around while your Josh and I take these two boys and have a little look around. But you may not be staying in this building very long."

Joining me, Josh and the two youths walked across my fields due west and came to my boundary. We spoke little. They were attempting to keep up with my pace and had already walked ten miles from dawn that day so we conveniently arrived with them out of breath and me with some ideas to discuss.

"Josh, what do you make of this land you see in front of you and what would you do with it? "

For the next ten minutes there was no sound, only eyes assessing every inch of that land and considering just what might be possible.

I had previously looked over the land many times and reached the conclusion that bought at a good price it could be vastly improved. Immediately below where we were standing a steady flow of water ran down the hill and gurgled its way west. Anywhere near the stream grass flourished, but over the rest of the large expanse it seemed arid and dry, little grass grew and as pasture it was sadly lacking. But it occurred to me that the stream could be partially diverted across the top of the land, drainage channels put in, so the flow of water would then permeate downhill to refresh the land and create a wonderful meadow. Would Josh see it in the same way?

Scratching his chin and talking slowly, Josh outlined his thoughts in a logical fashion, costing out the work and reaching exactly the conclusion I had come to.

I then asked formally if he would be willing to work for me and he answered with an immediate, "Yes."

That agreed I was about to return to the farm and outline my proposals when James, the eldest son, spoke up.

"Mr Rutherford, I have overheard your conversations with my father and wish to thank you very much for saving our family from ruin. May I put a thought to you, please?"

I told him to "Speak on." What transpired was very interesting, James had saved up very hard and had bought two gimmer lambs, to try and produce a small herd of sheep for the future. His ambition was to become a stone mason working out of York Minster and the apprenticeship was costly. The sale of the sheep would have met some of his fees.

Both his sheep had been stolen in the raid on the farm, but he asked if there was the possibility in the future to keep some sheep.

Now that coincided with some thoughts I had developed on sheep and I acted.

"James, that's a sound idea. We will buy two gimmers when we go to the mart. You look after them and build up a herd of sheep which I will buy from you when you are ready to go away to learn your trade. I reckon you are twelve years of age now and will be ready for work at age fourteen so can we come to an arrangement."

Much chin stroking followed, but then a broad smile came and, "Yes, Mr Rutherford, that would be grand."

We returned to the house at a much slower pace, discussing things all the way back. Once at my home I asked Josh to come in to my office and we agreed terms for his weekly wage and I gave him an immediate portion of his money to tide him over, plus a lot of the food we had.

I also asked if he had noticed the somewhat neglected farmhouse on the site we had just seen and of course that had been taken note of. "What would you say if I asked you to be tenant of that farmhouse and bring it up to reasonable standards for you to gradually move in and live there? I would agree with you a sum of money to be spent on the improvements and your family would be the tenants for as long as you work for me."

Josh looked long and hard at me. "I would like to think you will allow me six months to do all the necessary repairs and until then I hope you can agree I will live rent free. At the same time if the opportunity ever comes to purchase the house and some land I would like an agreement that I would have first refusal."

Very sound thinking on Josh's part, I thought, and just what I would have done. "Those are terms I can agree, Josh. Shake hands and we have a deal." Which we did.

"You and your family will have a roof over their heads

from now on but it will be the drovers' quarters for you all until I can buy that two hundred acres."

Outside there was a big commotion of horses neighing and people laughing and the rest of my family bounded into the house and took the place over again.

Giselle ran into my arms, as usual, laughing at my face as she displayed the parcels she had bought at the market and then suddenly realised we had guests.

Josh and his family were introduced and seemed completely bewitched by Giselle and her strange half French, half English accent such that they conversed long and all the girls seemed to get along very well on first acquaintance.

The general discussion and melee slowly settled down with the ladies all making for the house. Arthur was busily engaged removing the harness and rubbing down the horses whilst I noticed the two boys immediately helped to push the carriage into the covered yard.

Watching all this activity my eyes caught movement in the distance and I watched in some disbelief as a kilted figure strode up our long drive. This could only mean that a Scottish herd of cows and men would be needing a stance overnight and accommodation. Damn. This was very early in the season for cattle to be moving from Scotland and could only mean the farmers had hit hard times and needed the cash desperately. Or they had a rumour of good prices somewhere and I needed to know.

My business was now both farmer and drover and on this very substantial estate I now owned, we encouraged drovers to place their cattle in my fields overnight for some days and charged a halfpenny a beast. They were called Halfpenny fields in the business and I could make a good profit providing water and good pasture for the beasts and basic accommodation for the drovers.

But I had just given Josh and his family the drovers' accommodation and as they appeared in the distance a goodly number of men were in attendance.

Strolling up to the kilted Scotsman, I recognised him from previous visits and greeted him with a shake of the hand and a welcome nod and remembered his name was Angus.

"Och I'm glad to see you, Jack, and I hope you can accommodate me and my cattle and the lads?"

I told him it was no real problem and he mentioned about two hundred and twenty beasts would be coming along the road with ten men and as many dogs and that included four feisty young bulls. This stopped me in my tracks because the last thing I needed just before I left for France was problems with wild young bulls. I made it clear to the Scotsman that I could not afford any danger to me or my family and he would need to be extra vigilant particularly as the twenty two acre field had adequate fencing for docile weary cows but not for jumpy, active, randy bulls.

Josh had joined me now with his two boys and all parties nodded greetings to each other when I was pulled aside. "Jack, I have a knack of being able to calm feisty bulls just by quietly talking and singing to them and if this can be of help, you just have to say." This took me completely by surprise and with some quiet hope that it may be true we awaited the arrival of the herd.

I put them in the twenty two acre field and saw the four bulls had men at their heads and ropes attached to the copper rings in their noses with some having flecks of blood showing from constant heaving and prancing about. My worst fears were realised and with a heavy heart I was about to refuse entry to my cattle stance when Josh walked boldly over to the wild-looking bulls and despite the pleas of the minders to be careful he started to talk to these mad creatures.

Total silence fell as he muttered and talked to the creatures for a long time and they gradually ceased their cavorting about and grew calm and seemed to respond to his every word uttered in a sing song voice but hardly audible to us gaping bystanders. Gently he gathered the four halters and led these crazy bulls away as calm as could be to the absolute astonishment of the Scots drovers, and I.

"Och Jack, that's a rare talent yon man has, ye'll do very well with him on the books."

You could have heard a pin drop in the sudden silence that followed then the rest of the herd meekly followed where Josh led. Calm and peaceful they all entered the twenty two acre field and started grazing. I just could not believe my eyes and nor could our Scottish drovers. I had heard talk of men with this gift over animals but would never have given it credence until now.

Securely locking the gate and leaving Josh in the field to commune with his new friends, I asked the drovers to follow me to the accommodation they would use. At that point Angus mentioned they would like to stay overnight and the next day as well. He remarked on my excellent pasture and felt his cattle would benefit from a good feed and rest before they tackled the long road over Stainmore at this uncertain time of year.

I was questioned closely as we walked. I mentioned my success in Manchester and he asked for full details which I gave him. By this time we had all reached Ridley House and I asked the drovers and the two boys to wait while I discussed some matters with my wife.

Once I had explained my predicament, Giselle saw the problem immediately, thank goodness, and I noticed she and all the ladies were busy making tea and preparing a considerable amount of food. "Jack, I can see your dilemma and now we have discussed it. Margaret, Josh and the two boys will share two rooms at the top of the house while we all knuckle down and prepare the drovers' accommodation. I know it's early in the season but we all think we can get it ready for them. Margaret and her family can stay in here until they leave, and that's that!"

Powerful forces at work indoors are to be crossed at your personal peril, I have found from experience. I quickly retraced my steps and explained all to Angus and his men who immediately set off for the drovers' accommodation to help out, with me in attendance. Two hours of brushing and scrubbing with the ladies directing operations, and we had the place habitable. The drovers sat down to a substantial meal and the rest of us went into the house and prepared to tuck in. I grabbed some cooked meat and vegetables, put them in a metal pan and went out to the stance again.

Josh was still watching the bulls but in a very relaxed way and this demeanour had washed over onto the formerly feisty animals who now chewed the cud with the cows and looked remarkably settled and contented. Giving him the food, I suggested we slowly wander back to the house whilst I questioned him very closely about this strange ability of his.

He said, "It first became apparent about three years ago when I was in the Cattle Market in Kirby Stephen and a very wild angry bull was being brought to mart for sale. Nobody would have anything to do with it so I wandered over and just felt like talking to the damn thing, and bless me, it responded, to my surprise and all who witnessed it. From then on I was regularly called when a difficult animal was expected and I made a few shillings by being present at the sale and calming things down."

Music to my ears. Once I returned from France I would take Josh with me to Carlisle and see if he could work his charms on the crazy beast I now owned over there and for which I had a plan.

At the back of my mind was my intention to deal very severely with the lousy slimy beast who had intended to violate my Giselle as a so-called virgin bride. It rankled with me that, in spite of his status as a Magistrate, he could still get away with this foul charade and his professed knowledge of cattle might be used by me to ensure his downfall.

I kept this knowledge to myself for the time being and prepared myself for France. For the next week I was extremely busy, I arranged to purchase the two hundred acres next door and gave a substantial deposit for immediate possession of both the land and the farm. I asked Josh to accompany me to my Solicitors to make him aware of my intentions. I gave him clear instructions as to the placement of the revised watering system we had discussed in the fields and the repairs and improvements I expected to see to the farmhouse by the time I returned to England. I also gave him the money to buy two sheep, in lamb, for his son James as I promised.

By the end of that week, my affairs in reasonable order I took a reluctant leave of my beloved Giselle, young Giles and all my companions and workforce. I left having made it very clear to all concerned that in my absence Giselle's word was my word and law.

Early morning saw me bid farewell. riding a good horse and with a spare animal alongside. I carried my wallet with a lot of paper money and many gold sovereigns in a money belt secured with a large buckle as it appeared English gold was as good abroad as here. Minimum clothing was strapped on the spare horse with a weapon or two as well. I would sell the horses and then hire animals on my journey.

CHAPTER 11
HARWICH, GRAVELINES IN FRANCE

Riding hired horses in relays. I travelled along the Great North Road, turned to the left, passed Huntingdon and Cambridge and made the long journey to Harwich. I had thought of tasking a boat from Whitby or Hull but the much longer sea journey put me off and I decided to keep my exposure to the North Sea to a bare minimum, especially in April when it still looked grey and forbidding.

So after many days on the road I travelled the almost two hundred and sixty miles from Brough in Westmoreland to Sudbury in Suffolk and there I stayed with my very good friends in the White Horse Inn, Steven and Venetia. I brought them up to date on all my adventures and they asked about Giselle and my family and hoped that George Cook continued to prosper.

In the bar that night I questioned them closely about my chances of getting across to France and in particular to a quiet port handy for an inland journey. Of course they wanted to know all about the incident with the knife to Giselle's throat and entirely understood my reason for going to protect both our property and my wife's wellbeing.

Reliable locals were consulted and it became obvious that a lot of smuggling went on in the area and one place frequently mentioned was The Butt and Oyster tavern at Pin Mill. Brandy was brought ashore from France and English woollen fleeces were transported back in a strong and illicit trade.

Smuggling caught my attention because these good folk knew nothing of my other money-making activities and I preferred to keep it that way, but I cocked an ear and listened closely. Next morning, on a fresh horse and with many fond farewells I struck out across Suffolk to traverse the forty miles, making for Harwich as I told my friends but in reality making for Pin Mill and The Butt and Oyster. Two days later and a rough overnight stop saw me arrive at Pin Mill with its shallow harbour.

Quite late in the evening on a blustery day, I arrived in the area hoping to find a cheap and reliable form of ship to whip me quietly across the English Channel. I took a hearty meal in The Butt and Oyster tavern and by careful questioning found out that the odd smuggler came in late of an evening but was always gone by morning, strangely enough. So I enquired just where they might land or berth and after much discussion they hinted at the area I should visit. I let slip I was also a smuggler of tea and tobacco and that opened the conversation a lot.

Wandering down with all my meagre belongings on my back, I stood for a long time surveying the water and getting a feel for the place. It was certainly remote, with a small wooden landing stage and a very rough road nearby leading to goodness knows where across very flat land.

My eye was caught by a very lively vessel approaching across the water and making, in zig zags, for the landing I had spied earlier.

Strong winds from the south east buffeted the craft which I noted was handled by only two crew. Twice the vessel came up to the landing but to no avail. I moved on to the jetty and twice threw a rope as the vessel neared but the wind was far too strong.

Secured to the jetty was a serviceable small boat and I had noted a lot of rope nearby, so without more ado I created as long a stretch of rope as I could from the lengths around me then tied them to the jetty and allowed the boat, with me in it, to move offshore with the wind and I managed to get well out into the channel. The boat Captain spotted my intentions and came up in a long zig zag. Once he was close enough I threw him my last spare rope which he firmly attached to his vessel.

Then the real fun started. I had to haul them very slowly back towards the jetty but they eased my struggles very quickly by lowering all their sails and the elderly crewman leapt into the dinghy with me when he could and together we pulled and pulled and brought that boat right alongside the jetty where it was made secure. I was sweating profusely, as was the crewman. It took some time to get our breath back, at which moment the Skipper appeared on deck.

"Merci monsieur, possible une cognac avec moi."

This couldn't be better, a French cutter, doubtless a smuggler and hopefully going straight back to France. But where?

On board the sailor wiped imaginary sweat from his brow, waved me on to his boat with a cry of "Entre" to which I acted promptly, asked for permission to come aboard where we shook hands and went into a small but comfortable cabin.

Two substantial glasses of cognac appeared. We eyed each other carefully and took a drink of a very nice drop of alcohol.

"Je m'appel Serge, et vous."

Now Giselle had hammered in to my brain a smattering of French sufficient for me to respond, "Jack."

That brought a ready smile to a man who stood, like me, about 6ft tall, well built and weatherbeaten, aged, I guessed about twenty four or five. Swarthy faced, with a gold earring, fancy red cloth around his neck and wearing a sailors smock and serge trousers. If this bloke wasn't a smuggler I would be most surprised.

So nothing ventured as they say... I said, "I am a smuggler of tea and tobacco. What do you deal in?"

Slapping his knee, downing his brandy in one huge gulp and laughing fit to burst, he refilled our glasses and in halting English told me he was, indeed, a smuggler and had a valuable cargo to unload before he sailed back to France. Was I willing to help him please as he was desperately shorthanded. He had sailed from Gravelines near Dunkirk two days ago and was delivering, very late, a load of contraband brandy and silk to a local dealer who would pay cash.

Immediately I agreed, more brandy was taken and my liking for this French entrepreneur deepened. We had a lot in common. Night had drawn in and Serge repeated his assignment ashore now that darkness had fallen. Would I assist? Of course.

Shortly and quietly a horse and trap turned up, well muffled with cloth around all jingling harness and we started some very hard work. The crewman lifted the boxes from the hold on to the deck, I moved them from the deck to the shore then Serge manhandled them to the dealer who placed them in his trap. For a full twenty minutes we worked without a break and I found it hard graft, but as we finished I noticed Serge was almost dropping with fatigue so I went to his side and gave him a hand into his boat from the jetty where I noticed he had been paid what appeared to be a lot of money. Back on board we saw the dealer move away in to the night.

Serge then stated he had left port two days ago and had sailed without rest all the way to Harwich to meet his deadline with the dealer. He was now dropping with fatigue and tiredness yet he could not take a break as he had to leave immediately to be out of sight of Harwich by morning,

Much as I was willing to help, I held my counsel and listened to what could be a route to France from England. Serge looked long and hard at me as we assessed each other's likely abilities and it was then that I decided to commit to the venture.

In my halting French and English I explained that I had business in Saint Omer where my wife's late parents had been murdered. Some bastard was claiming inheritance and needed talking to. I also mentioned the knife to Giselle's throat and the demand that she sign away her inheritance.

Serge's brow darkened. He was not surprised at my wish to meet the French usurper and suggested he could possibly be of use in the negotiations but in return he begged a favour from me. He now knew I was a drover of cattle over long distances and used to orienteering on land. This made him suggest that I accompany him on his voyage to France and steer the boat on a course he would set. All I had to do was keep to that course while he took at least three hours' sleep.

Goodness knows what possessed me but I agreed. I liked the man even on such a short acquaintance. He was in my own mould and somebody I could easily get along with. It boded well but first of all we had to cross the English Channel.

I was introduced to the gnarled fisherman who was crew and was delighted to shake the hand of Jean Pierre du Parc with whom I had hauled this damned boat to the jetty. We had slipped the formalities of an introduction in the vigorous activity of heaving on rope.

Setting sail, the favourable south west wind took us out of the harbour on the River Stour and towards the town of Harwich where we took the headland very wide, turned roughly south west and manoeuvred past the Naze Flats and out into the English Channel.

Breaking waves now appeared which the boat took easily, thank goodness. This vessel, the Nimrod, was wooden built, about 45ft long and 14ft wide with a single mast, a sail at the bows, a jib in English terms I learned, plus a large main sail on what I found out was a gaff rig. Serge showed me all the sheets and halyards as they are named although what the French terms are I had no idea.

No lights were carried of course, so we sailed in to a stygian gloom where occasionally I could see white water as waves broke nearby. Our rocking motion increased but so did our pace and a steady flow of water under the transom gurgled loudly at our progress. We had a compass I was glad to see and this was lit in a binnacle by a very small candle so I could just make out the apparent direction from the compass needle.

Serge indicated I maintain and keep rigidly to a course of 123 degrees which would take us to, by his reckoning, Gravelines where we would hopefully land.

I asked if wind and tide would wreak havoc with this heading but I gathered he thought our passage would be so slow all tidal movement up and down the coast would be negated. He was the mariner but I thought this a somewhat relaxed approach to a sea passage.

It's about one hundred sea miles as the crow flies from Harwich to Gravelines and at four knots per hour I hoped that Serge and Jean Pierre would get their heads down and have at least four hours' sleep before dawn and a reassessment of our location. So down into the cabin and heads down and both were out like babies, leaving me in charge. Blustery showers came and went and in their midst we had little or no visibility but just charged on relentlessly. Becoming accustomed to the motion I found myself enjoying the freedom and this new exciting experience, certainly when the wind freshened I had the confidence to reduce the sails a little as I had been instructed and our heeling motion in the water reduced dramatically to a more upright position but our speed did not appear to diminish.

On into the dark night, glancing frequently at the compass I maintained the course of 123 degrees and I relaxed a little, my many nights guarding cattle giving me the stamina to stay awake and alert and I let my thoughts wander to my course of action once we landed. If I could persuade Serge to accompany me, I would have a welcome ally and I suspected a formidable warrior.

Splashing water brought me alert and as the sound increased so did my alarm until a black apparition came straight for our craft and would have completely swamped us had I not turned the tiller quickly to the left. A vast wheel on the side of a massive boat brushed our flimsy craft aside.

Straight after came the stern and a large wave caused by the passing of this craft. My prompt action with the tiller had turned the head of the boat into the waves and prevented us being almost swamped. There was water everywhere sloshing about and we made a sickening side to side motion that had me gripping the tiller for support.

An angry looking figure appeared in the cabin door and demanded an explanation. I just pointed at the sparks, ashes and steam coming from the huge boat that had nearly run us down and he needed no further detail.

"le Diable! le Diable! Mon Dieu qu'est-ce c'est? le Diable?"

Then "Mon Dieu" was muttered loudly as the cabin door shut and I was left, visibly shaken, to continue navigating so I concentrated on bringing the boat back onto the 123 degrees heading which took some time.

Mulling over the experience during the next three hours it occurred to me that must have been one of the new steam paddle boats I had read about in the newspapers. It was an awesome sight and bigger than anything I had previously seen and of course with that steam engine it was not affected by wind direction and could leave harbour at will.

That thought process stayed with me for the rest of the night until way after dawn I woke Serge and Jean Pierre who both looked a damned sight better than they had when they went to bed and despite the incident in the night both had slept very well.

We had left Harwich at about midnight and it was now 7am so we had made about twenty eight to thirty sea miles of our journey. Through that day and into the night, taking turns on the tiller, we reached Gravelines at about 4am. Serge was certain that there would be a watch out for his boat as the Customs were taking a much greater interest in him than previously and we were warned to be extremely vigilant. As luck would have it, two large English warships passed close to the Fort Grand Phillipe and a single warning shot was fired to ward the English off. French Customs had a boat on watch, but it ran due south once the English warships appeared, at least that's the impression we had in the very limited light.

Serge seized the opportunity and steered our boat straight at the harbour entrance as quickly as possible, where we slipped the boat into a very secluded, quiet part of the harbour and having tied up, leapt onto the small jetty.

Ashore again with the boat secured and Serge shushing me with a gesture, I grabbed my bag and hurriedly followed Serge and Jean Pierre on a path heading for houses and a café. It was dimly lit but busy even at that dark moment before dawn.

All my considerable money was in English pounds plus small coins and I knew Serge was paid in English money as I had seen the large wad of notes he received in Harwich, so I broached the subject of changing my money into francs. He just tapped his finger on the side of his nose and bade me follow him into the warm muggy atmosphere of a scruffy, typically fisherman's, early morning haunt.

Serge was greeted warmly on all sides but my appearance and clothing left no doubt I was English and there was a certain wariness. England had defeated

France at Waterloo just six years earlier and there was still an apparent animosity.

Finding a spare table, Serge ordered some food for us both and some coffee, which was a new one on me but I suspected tea would be in very short supply here.

Toasted bread with a generous helping of cheese was served with a dark liquid that I guessed was the coffee drink. Although very thirsty, tired out and desperate for sleep, I ate the toast but watched carefully until I saw Serge heap a great spoonful of sugar into his drink and savour it, so I followed suit. As the hot liquid ran down my throat I felt a burst of energy flow through my body and gradually my weariness reduced a little.

Waving me to follow, Serge led the way through a curtain into a much smaller room which appeared to be an office of sorts and behind a desk a swarthy man, not unlike Serge, rose, grinned conspiratorially and kissed him on both cheeks whilst shaking hands. Somewhat surprised I waited to be greeted and to my embarrassment, the same performance took place, but this appeared to be normal for a greeting.

I understood at least half of the conversation that followed and got the impression that a hard bargain was being struck to change our money into French francs. Ten minutes of trading in a smoke-filled office eventually saw me part with some of my English money in return for a huge wad of French francs in various denominations. I pocketed my money, did the goodbye thing, then came back into the café intent on paying our bill.

Some big loutish half pissed French youth grabbed my lapel, shouted, "Mal Anglais," and tried to take a swipe at me. I nodded to Serge to clear a space, kneed the man in the crotch and nutted him on his nose as he passed me on his way down to the floor. Then I drew my dagger and held it to his throat and asked in French for an apology, which he stuttered out.

Standing and replacing my dagger, I noticed it had gone very quiet in the room, with Serge grinning and standing over me to prevent interference. He too had a dagger in his hand.

It was rough company, I thought, but we paid our dues and strode out into the beginnings of dawn. We were both now shattered with tiredness, the adrenaline of the fight dissipating quickly. I needed sleep very soon. We walked quickly through the lightening streets and came to a fishermen's cottage area where we stopped at a door. Serge unlocked it and we went indoors where a lady appeared, hugged Serge, looked at me curiously then started boiling water.

It seemed Serge was not very popular with his wife who didn't know of his recent dash to England and had been worried sick about his safety. Suddenly two small children dashed into the room and dived on their seated father and chattered loudly in great excitement. This brought a smile to his wife's face. She came to me, held my hand and whispered, "Je m'appelle Sylvie. Je suis la femme de Serge."

I made myself known in my halting French and we actually

kissed and shook hands. Sylvie was simply gorgeous, petite, dark haired and as I came to know her, very wise counsel. Once I had explained that my wife, Giselle, was French the whole conversation centred on how we met.

Serge stopped this talk short. We took to the stairs and I collapsed into a very solid sleep, waking at about 7pm where we enjoyed a very full meal that Sylvie had prepared for us. Then we planned how I might achieve my objective in Saint Omer. I explained the activities of the so-called illegitimate bastard who had tried to have Giselle's throat cut, who I intended to confront.

Eyes lighting up at the thought of trouble, Serge suggested, to my delight, that he would accompany me and help stir up the local criminal populace who rumour had it were not nice people.

We eventually retired for more much needed sleep, resolving to have an early start on hired horses and make our way to Saint Omer.

All my droving instincts came to my rescue when, deep into the night I thought I heard very quiet noises outside my window. Peering out without lighting a candle I stared for some long time and thought I was hearing things but slowly, as my eyes adjusted, I made out the occasional glint from a blade or uniform badge. Suspicious now, I stole through to the main bedroom and woke Serge and asked him to follow me. Once he had seen the activity below he became animated. "It is the Customs men come to arrest me. They came today when we were out but Sylvie told them we were gone."

Great news! Moving quickly, finding our weapons and warm clothing I followed Serge into the roof space. There he lifted four pan tiles from the roof and created a space wide enough for us to crawl out. He bade me, very quietly, to remove my boots and tie them behind my back. We then crept slowly out and on the roof where we slid across five houses before dropping to the ground via some lean-to sheds. All was quiet. We donned our boots and crept slowly through the town until we came to a fisherman's cottage where we knocked and went in.

Serge mentioned he had been under suspicion for a very long time by the Customs who now, it appeared, had sufficient proof to arrest him. They had enlisted the help of soldiers from the Grand Fort Phillipe which was nearby and only through my habitual wariness had we avoided capture as I was certain I would be included in any arrests.

Once safely inside that fisherman's house, I learned the true enormity of Serge's difficulties. From the whispered conversation, it appeared Serge was being constantly watched. The Customs men had arrested the merchant who had sold him the illicit brandy, and rumour then had it that he had admitted his part in the affair and thus Serge's arrest was arranged. But by some fluke of weather or darkness, we had successfully made the safety of the harbour, and our only point of contact before going to his house was the café where we changed our coin.

Sure enough our fisherman friend confirmed that the stupid youth who had tried to steal my money had immediately run to the Customs office and told them of our arrival. That would have to be dealt with although the fisherman reckoned the man's days in town were very numbered. Serge's boat had been seized already and was being stripped down to the keel at that very moment, so this meant his livelihood as a fisherman and smuggler had come to an abrupt end.

For a man whose life and income prospects were now very reduced, Serge took the blow with an immense shrug and remained silent for a long time.

Then from his pocket he drew some English sovereigns worth a hell of a lot of francs in this coastal area and readily accepted as payment for goods and services. He gave these to his friend to give to Sylvie at the earliest possible moment to enable her to go about her daily routine and pay her bills. By my reckoning she would be able to cope for two months at least from the amount I saw passed over.

By now I had francs in a leather bag about my neck hidden under my shirt but I also carried English gold sovereigns in great number and a couple of small diamonds hidden in my money belt, so we were reasonably prepared.

At my suggestion, we agreed to leave immediately for Saint Omer and our fisherman friend suggested we waited till the outskirts of Gravelines before we attempted to buy two horses for the journey.

Moving as silently as possible through the dark streets, we avoided military patrols near the fort and made our way out of town on a recommended route via the canal that apparently ran from Gravelines to Saint Omer.

CHAPTER 12
SAINT OMER, FRANCE

After steady riding on our hired horses, we approached Saint Omer in the late evening. We found a tavern with accommodation, enjoyed a very nice meal then woke the next morning ready for action.

First step was to find the Hotel de Ville and talk to the Mayor, who eventually agreed to see us but with some reluctance. The battle of Waterloo still loomed large in the French psyche and animosity hung in the air as we entered his smart office but the sight of an obviously French man accompanying me eased matters a little. So I told my tale and the Mayor listened with growing alarm to the facts I placed before him. Pausing to order coffee to be served, he quietly condensed my details and suggested we had certain priorities.

First was to establish where M. and Madam Durrand, the former chemists, were buried and I was surprised when the Mayor announced where the cemetery was and that the gravestone had been erected and paid for by public subscription.

Next I was asked to produce evidence of my marriage

to Giselle and thankfully Dyson Frobisher had created a written note on his Solicitor's letter heading, but of course in English, confirming the date and time of our wedding in Brough, Westmoreland. After much head scratching and deliberation in a mixture of French and English, our new common language, this document was accepted as proof.

When I suggested I would like to look at the property, a long pause came in proceedings until slowly and with a little embarrassment the Mayor confessed he had allowed the illegitimate supposed son of M. Durrand to take over the building. He had received a letter from people known in the area to act in suspicious ways suggesting that in the absence of any known dependents, the Durrand estate should pass to this man, the imposter and they would occupy the building immediately to 'protect it', this despite the Mayor telling me he had received Giselle's letter some time ago but these imposters had insisted it was a forgery.

Wringing his hands in despair, the Mayor hinted we were against up against some dirty tricks people who would take action against our interference.

Leaving the Mayor's office, Serge and I strolled round the town getting a feel for what turned out to be a very vibrant and pleasant place. We stopped at a hardware store and purchased further long swords and cudgels. Firearms were available but we merely noted their presence for the future.

I explained to Serge that this was going to get very messy and he may wish to bow out, but after he used strong language to insist on his involvement I got the distinct impression he was as excited at the prospect of battle as I was.

So we came to our property in Place Victor Hugo, a large stone building four stories high and set on a corner of the square with a narrow alley type thoroughfare running to the left of the structure and known as rue Clouteries.

From our first view of the property I could see the size of the structure with a broad frontage and down the side route there was access to the rear and doors leading to upper rooms. It was of a substantial size and the former chemist's shop was now closed with the front door firmly locked.

Serge and I wandered to the rear of the building and whilst nobody was watching, we forced open the rear door, stepped into the gloomy interior and carefully closed the door behind us. There were footsteps on the floor above but they appeared to come from one person and we crept slowly forward, allowing our eyes to became accustomed to the dim light.

Moving slowly we found ourselves in a short passageway leading to the main shop premises where many of the counters and fittings had been stripped from the walls but had not yet been removed.

Footsteps neared and we watched and waited as a rear door was slowly opened and not one but three figures appeared in the room staring menacingly at us.

"Quel que vous faissez ici!" demanded the first man to

enter and I replied, "I own the bloody place," in English of course. Serge grinned as he translated this message.

Things happened very quickly from there. They flew at us in great anger but we were ready. Using the heavy cudgels we bought earlier, we swung into action with terrific speed and Serge was quite the man of war I had anticipated. He had two men down before I could blink but I had by far the bigger of the ruffians and had a hard battle on my hands before I overcame him with underhand blows to his midriff and legs, a smashing fist into his face and a final knockout blow to the back of his neck but not before I had taken a few heavy blows to my face and arms.

Serge, both his men laid low and unconscious at his feet, had taken no part in my struggle with a very big and broad man, in fact he had watched the whole proceedings with an interested grin on his face but no offer of assistance. I commented on this as we secured our assailants with some cloth from their apparel but he reckoned I was doing alright and he didn't want to spoil my fun.

Following this friendly exchange, Serge questioned these men and they were apparently there as guardians of the property for the new owner, Guillaume Ribauld, who I knew as the supposed illegitimate son of Giselle's father, Gerard Durrand.

Further pressure from Serge and it was revealed that Monsieur Ribauld was a well known young tearaway in the area whose brother worked for the Mayor in the

Hotel de Ville. So now we knew how the information had been obtained following Giselle's letter to the Mayor. It also transpired Ribauld brought fear and terror to the area by using five ex-British soldiers as his strongmen and was widely feared.

I needed resolution here very quickly as I was anxious to settle these affairs to my satisfaction and return to England. With this thought, I whispered to Serge we should let these men go, let them report what they had seen but that we would wait until night time to release them and follow them to their destination.

Darkness saw us rough these men up a little more then we freed them with the reminder that if we saw them again they were dead. They were not to report what they had seen to anybody.

We moved quickly to follow them after they had left, checked our weapons, locked the door as best we could and followed at a distance from the fast moving villains. Sure enough they made straight for the unsavoury part of town. We followed carefully and surreptitiously because they frequently glanced back as they made their way. After a long walk we saw them enter a two storey street house which we marked carefully in our minds. Serge and I then went to ground and considered our options. If the information we had was correct, then five ex-British Army thugs would be too much for us to tackle but if we could separate them and tackle them individually, we could wear down the opposition to a less formidable force.

CHAPTER 13
BATTLE IN STREET

We knew the British Army of old and could practically guarantee they would need drink, and copious quantities of it so we scouted about a little, found a suitable café, had a meal and Serge charmed our waitress such that she let slip the "Mal Anglais Militaire" regularly drank in the nearby tavern.

We needed accommodation as a priority but deemed it wise to leave this vicinity.

Securing lodgings well away, we then returned to see what might happen.

Securely lodged in a small café where Serge seemed to know some people, we changed into dark clothing and gathered our cudgels and short swords which we hid under our clothing. We retraced our steps and entered the tavern the young waitress had indicated. I asked Serge to handle all the conversation and I would play dumb. Serge ordered two large glasses of red wine.

We sat in a corner to watch the proceedings and the quiet murmur of voices started afresh once we had sat down. There was no undue interest in our presence.

We slowly drank our wine, talking quietly about ourselves and I was very interested to hear that Serge's wife's family farmed extensively in the area and would be well placed to advise on the considerable land holdings that it appeared the Durrand family owned in the area. This was most interesting news to me and Serge suggested a second round of drinks which he approached the bar to purchase but as he rose two big rough men appeared and demanded beer in loud English voices.

All conversation stopped, men drank their wine and edged nervously towards the door to leave and the landlord was petrified and shaking as he served them. With two large glasses of beer apiece they took seats near where I was sitting and quaffed a pint straight down. Serge collected our wine and returned to our table but not before he had moved the table to make a quick move into action. I had done the same because from their loud conversation these were two of the thugs employed by Ribauld and we needed to remove them from the field of future battle.

It was almost too easy really. They took exception to Serge and the fact he drank wine not beer and taunted him in English for a few long moments until I told them to, "Keep bloody quiet, you lousy shits," and that had entirely the right effect. By this time they'd had, by my reckoning, about four pints of beer in them and bravado at their local reputation was enough for them to try to lunge out of their seats to deal with us. We were both out of our seats and on them with our cudgels.

They had no idea what was happening. We broke both their arms and smashed their knees once we had them suitably wounded and we showed no mercy at all. It was ruthless.

We needed them out of the equation permanently and quick thinking by Serge saw him suggest to the owner that these men should be locked up by the local watchmen. Quickly they were placed in wheelbarrows and taken to gaol with the landlord's written testimony that they had attacked us first.

Finishing our drinks and with the good wishes of the landlord ringing in our ears, we left by a side door and commenced our journey to our accommodation. But I had a niggling feeling we were being followed and by cutting through a dark alley and doubling back we saw a burly man creeping to where we had last been standing, and he had a big cudgel.

Watching his movements, he became aware we were not in the position he expected us to be and was scratching his head and cursing (that's what gave him away). It was good old English swear words. I walked up to the man directly and asked why he was following me at which he strode forward with his cudgel raised when Serge thumped him on his back and he dropped like a stone to the rough ground. We broke his arms and made his knee very misshapen with our own cudgels and left him whimpering on the ground. That left Ribauld and two men which we reckoned was about right so we found our way to our lodgings and had a good rest because tomorrow the hornets' nest would erupt.

Morning saw us both back at the premises in Place Victor Hugo where we entered again and this time opened the front door to see and be seen. We had removed our swords to appear non-threatening and it was pleasant to stand in the sunshine and bring light into the big store. Curious bystanders gathered to ask if we were opening again but we gently explained this was just a first glimpse at our new property and a scruffy man on the edge of the crowd quickly ran away with that news. Within moments two burly men shouldered their way through the crowd and created a space in front of us. From the crowd a foppish well-dressed dandy appeared, waved all the crowd to stand back and demanded to know who dared to enter his father's house.

I came forward and in my halting French suggested he was a cheating bastard as Mr Durrand, my wife's father, had been impotent after her birth and he was an imposter. My intention was to rile him into attacking me when I hoped to work off my frustrations on him and put a knife to his throat.

A large crowd had gathered and I noticed the Mayor standing nervously by, wringing his hands, well aware now that his position in the town had drawn unfavourable comparisons.

Strangely, at the back of the crowd, a uniformed British Officer, mounted on a magnificent horse was watching proceedings with great interest.

Shouting to make myself heard and with Serge translating I reiterated I was the husband of Giselle, the daughter of the late Gerard and Benedickte Durrand, and I had shown the Mayor my Certificate of Marriage. Further, I was aware that Giselle's father had contracted oreillons shortly after her birth and he was infertile. From the age of this usurper he was younger than Giselle's twenty years.

This was received with gasps of amazement from the gathering crowd who started murmuring angrily at Ribauld who then completely lost his head in wild anger. Throwing off his fancy coat, he produced a long steel rapier and commenced an attack on me of a ferocity I have rarely witnessed and I appeared to him to be unarmed. Dancing quickly away from his thrusting blade, I received a sharp cut to my left arm which bled immediately. Reaching down, I found my dagger and was prepared to defend myself to the death despite the fearsome long reach of the weapon that Ribauld held.

We danced around and I deliberately lost ground to him hoping he would tire but that didn't happen. He grinned and thrust again and again shouting, "Die Englishman, Die," but I had no intention of doing so and then he slipped on the cobbles. I was about to take advantage when one of his cohorts grabbed me from behind and held me until my assailant rose again.

But in that pause, the English officer forced his mount through the massive crowd and as the thug let me go, he threw me his Lancers' curved sword which I caught and turned to repel a most savage attack on me which I parried now with a much more sinister weapon.

Ribauld was beside himself with fury and commenced a series of swipes and slashes that would have killed me instantly had it not been for the fine weapon I was now handling and getting used to.

Ribauld eventually tired, as I knew he would. Mine is a hard life and I am extremely strong and fit so I gradually overcame the savage attacks and started to fight back at my assailant who for the first time since we commenced this long battle showed an inkling of fear in his eyes.

Mercilessly I stood my ground, beat off every challenge and then went on the attack taking blows on my body but nothing compared to the damage I now did to the upstart. Starting with his shoulders, I savaged him until he bled from both arms and took a lot of punishment from me.

In my mind's eye was the image of my Giselle with a knife to her throat. I was merciless. Finally in desperation, he jumped in the air to deliver what he hoped was the coupe de gras but I took the opportunity whilst he was airborne to slash his stomach open and I split him right through. He died instantly. Screams from the assembled crowd and blood flying in all directions, I lowered the sword and in a brief lull wiped it carefully.

Serge had taken control by then. He floored the two cutthroats that Ribauld had brought with him and the crowd stood in shocked silence as I walked to the British Officer, wiped his blade again on my sweat soaked smock, handed him the sword by the hilt and thanked him for the kind gesture. He nodded and quietly asked if he could call on me the next morning to which I agreed.

There was a dead body on the Square and many witnesses. Serge told me afterwards that the Mayor declared that I had been set upon by a notoriously skilled swordsman who had killed twice before in similar circumstances and was entirely free of blame.

At that moment I couldn't have cared less, I was absolutely exhausted so Serge and I entered the building I now owned and sat on the floor for two hours as I recovered.

My injuries seemed to be a deep cut to my left leg, a gash on my left arm and a fair loss of blood. Serge ripped his clothing to clean the wounds as best he could then bandaged them securely.

When we next ventured outside, the body had gone, the streets were clean, the crowd had gone and a note on the door asked me to attend at the Mayor's rooms next afternoon to complete the transfer of land to my name.

CHAPTER 14
FRENCH PROPERTY DEAL

After an evening bathing my wounds and re-bandaging them with Serge's help, we woke next morning and entered the former chemist's shop that now looked somewhat forlorn. I had made Serge aware that the estate also included a large amount of land used we believed as pasture and we agreed we should view it.

So from our early start we travelled south on our horses and found what we believed would be my land if it was so proved. There was considerable potential that I could see as an experienced farmer but it was in France, not England. It was my belief that once you acquire land you should try to put it to use and consider it a long term investment. I was greatly taxed with these thoughts when Serge nudged me and suggested we might talk.

We dismounted and talked. Serge explained that he was now without any income. He could not return to Gravelines as he would be immediately arrested for smuggling and he had a wife and family to support. He made me aware that he had relatives in the area who were farmers on both his and his wife's side and indeed he had briefly considered farming as a career but the excitement of smuggling won hands down. Or it had.

He suggested he could become the Agent of my estate in France and would be prepared to invest some of his own money into the venture if I was willing to trust him. For the next hour we thoroughly explored the proposal and I deliberately pushed him very hard to explain just what he would do, how he would do it and how I would benefit. He refused to answer but demanded that I should give him at least one day to consider all I had suggested. Then he would give me his proposals after he had carefully mulled it over.

This was the best answer I could hope for and we mounted and returned to Saint Omer to find the British Officer just arrived for our meeting. Local boys took our horses to stables and we moved to a nearby café for a welcome glass of wine.

Major Basil Rathbone introduced himself to us and I thanked him again for his prompt action that had saved my life. He confessed he had a deep ulterior motive in my survival. He was a Military Surgeon and Doctor married to a French widow and he had firm intentions to settle in the region of Saint Omer. For many weeks he had tried to rent the former chemist's shop I now owned but he became aware, from contacts, that all was not well with the proven ownership of the business and he had kept a close watch on developments. He was present, of course, when I goaded the upstart Ribauld into fighting with me.

That was at the back of his mind when he threw me

his sword but he also admired my skill in avoiding instant death at the hands of a skilled swordsman with a sharp rapier against my small dirk.

Plus I was English which swayed him in my favour.

Without more ado I introduced myself and my French Agent Monsieur Serge Dubois who would conduct all negotiations immediately. I'll say this for Serge, who went up in further in my estimation, he didn't blink, just started enquiring how long a lease was anticipated, would Basil (for we were now on first name terms) wish to live on the premises and how many horses did he need stabling for. Dates were discussed and in my presence, a very handsome deal was struck, hands shaken and Basil left, a very happy man.

Serge and I then had to agree terms which took the rest of the morning and two more glasses of wine plus lunch but at the end of the discussion I felt very comfortable with the deal.

Immediately we visited a bank in the Square and eventually made ourselves known. The bank manager was very standoffish and haughty until I removed twenty gold English sovereigns from my money belt and laid them before him on his desk.

His demeanour changed at once, wine glasses were produced and our new bank account was established.

I suggested Serge and his family would move in to the main house once the chemist's shop was established and he proposed to let the rear half of the building which included two rooms below and two above plus a dressing area which would bring further income.

Additionally he would take over the huge area of pasture once we confirmed its exact location to run that as a farm, rear cattle and grow wheat and barley.

He would invest no money in the Estate but would manage its affairs to produce a profit in two years time which we would share equally after all agreed expenses. I in my turn expected quarterly progress reports and copies of bank statements which was a new one to Serge but he agreed, this would all be posted to me regularly. I would visit again in two years' time.

We didn't have time for a drink to toast our new arrangement as we had to be at the Mayor's office almost immediately so we hurried out after paying our bill.

Mayor's offices appear to be built to overwhelm visitors but on this occasion the Mayor came charging out of his room to greet us with stupid kisses and gave his grateful thanks that we had managed between us to rid the town of a very troublesome crowd of people. As we were speaking, a subdued man was led from the building in chains to be tried for stealing papers from the Mayor's office.

With the huge authority granted to Mayors in France under the Napoleonic Code, my marriage lines had been verified and accepted and it was now written in law that I was the owner of the late Gerard Durrand's Estate by virtue of my marriage to his only daughter Giselle. That was a load off my mind.

Serge Dubois was then formally introduced as my estate manager to whom all matters pertaining to the land

and buildings would now be addressed. The Mayor was somewhat surprised at this announcement until Serge told him to whom he was related, locally.

A very different approach became apparent. There would be no recriminations from me after the letter from my wife had 'gone missing' but Serge gently made it clear the matter remained on his personal file 'just in case' which the Mayor took with some relief.

Finally the Mayor confirmed that the joint burial had taken place after a full funeral service in the Saint Sepulchre Church which I knew would please Giselle immensely.

CHAPTER 15
KIRK SEEN IN FRANCE

It puzzled me greatly that there may be a connection between the knife incident at my house, the sudden appearance of an illegitimate so-called brother and knowledge of the valuable estate owned by the Durrand's.

One name kept coming back to me and that was Silas Kirk who had knowledge of the Durrand business, who had dubious contacts from his days in France and whose cutthroats had appeared as the guardians of the late Ribauld. Could he be behind all this business and using his contacts to engineer my downfall? I would not be in the least surprised and I resolved to make some discreet enquiries before I left for England.

Serge had suggested I use one of his contacts in Gravelines to take me out to the sea and catch a voyage to Hull or a North Sea port in a returning Herring Fleet boat that would be moving back north at that time of year. It would cost me some money but I had enough left and more to cover that expense.

With thoughts of an early return to Giselle and my family, I strolled round the pleasant streets of Saint

Omer, on my own, alert and watchful as always and my eye was caught by a young maiden being dragged kicking into an alley. This was familiar to me and I raced to the spot I had last seen her but to no avail, no trace. I moved on a little further and caught another glimpse of the frenzied maiden, kicking and fighting, and I went forward to investigate.

You would think by now that I had enough sense to spot a trap such as this, but I was reminded of my Giselle and her plight and I moved straight in to the trap that that bastard Kirk had laid for me.

Entering the alley I was seized from behind and a sack placed over my head, then I heard, "Surprised you, have I, Mr Rutherford? Still trying to rescue young maidens in distress? This, I am determined, will be the death of you." It was the voice of Silas Kirk.

I was bundled unceremoniously down the alley and pushed into a side opening where my hands were securely fastened and the sack was removed from my head.

Silas Kirk stood in the narrow space with two other men, one holding the frantically struggling girl who stared in horror as I was given a sound thrashing with blows to my face, arms, legs and stomach until I fell soundless to the floor and saw to my horror my faithful dagger slide across the narrow space. Suffering kicks to my ribs and back, I squirmed and twisted away with each blow to lessen the impact. Kirk drew a knife, approached me on limping legs and attempted to cut my throat but I anticipated the blow and kicked him hard on his leg, which buckled under him.

We ended up lying face to face on the ground, two of his men sat on me. He raised his hand holding the knife against which I had no defence and waited to die when a piercing scream shattered the sound.

My missing dagger had been found and used with good effect on the back of one of my assailants whose face contorted and with a whirl of skirts the feisty young maiden was off down the street.

"Stop her," shouted Kirk, rolling off me and staggering upright in an ungainly way. "Stop her, you idiots, that's good money escaping."

Quickly rising, the unhurt ruffian raced out of the alley, straight into a crowd of people drawn by the commotion. He stopped. Then fled, followed by his injured companion.

That left me bound still on the ground. Kirk lashed out a vicious kick and then scrambled up and left, swearing that I had a charmed bloody life but he would kill me soon.

"I know where you live," he shouted, "and I know you have a son, he will be next!"

That really scared me.

Out of the crowd, people came to my aid, released my hands and carefully supported me on the shoulders of two men who took me to our premises in Victor Hugo Street.

Serge was still in discussion with the returned Major Rathbone who, on seeing my plight immediately called for bandages, water and other equipment which he carried in a pannier on his nearby horse.

I couldn't have been in better hands and within an hour I was taking a small sip of watered wine and recounting the story of my thorough thrashing at the hands of Silas Kirk.

Major Basil knew all about Kirk and his cutthroats and agreed he would contact local British Army units still in the area to detain him for questioning but we knew that was a remote possibility.

That evening Serge and I sat in a local bar, me drinking watered wine as we discussed at length what we should do next.

It was now imperative that I return to England and my family but I knew it would take three more days of rest at least before I dare travel. My plan was to travel on horseback to Gravelines, give Serge's wife Amelie some money to arrange to leave their rented house, hire a horse and wagon and quietly come to Saint Omer. Then take advice from the fishermen to see if my plan to catch a returning herring boat would work.

Serge's bombshell came out of the blue.

"Amelie will not agree, of course, and you will never get her to leave Gravelines without a furious and protracted fight. I have suggested it many times as the Customs and Revenue men watched my activities but she was adamant. You are a very brave man to attempt it, but give her my love."

Some friend. Over the next two days I struggled round the area, ever watchful now for Kirk, but nothing untoward happened. Each day Serge attended at the chemist's shop and arranged for chosen workmen of good reputation to carry out the work of restoring the chemist's shop section, painting and decorating the interior room he intended to use and overseeing the installation of tenants in the letting room at the rear. Each evening after dinner he took a horse and checked the pasture land he now managed, grass was mown and dried, cattle were introduced to the fertile ground on a rental basis and I grew more and more confident that my smuggler friend was indeed a very shrewd business man.

It struck me as very strange that he had chosen to paint and decorate the large rooms above the shop where he proposed his family would live. I must confess that having struggled up the stairs on my final day I ran into plenty of hard working painters and the choice of colours was excellent.

Unable to keep quiet any longer I put the point to Serge. "This is a hell of a lot of effort in decoration for a set of rooms you say Amelie will never agree to use."

Cheeky bugger just tapped the side of his nose and gave me a knowing wink.

Then it dawned on me, both he and Amelie had family and friends in this area and some indeed in the town. Of course all the artisans working inside were well known to him and word would be passed that "Serge is making a wonderful home for some lucky lady." My conversations with Amelie may not be as difficult as I imagined

It was mid July when I left England to come to France and resolve any difficulties and at times it seemed as though I had been here forever. But hard reality now stepped in; days had passed very quickly and I realised it was now almost September. Battered as I was I was needed at home.

Mounting my horse and trailing a further one, I bade goodbye and headed for Gravelines which I reached two weary and painful days later.

Reluctantly I knocked on the door of Serge and Amelie's house when I arrived in the town late at night. I was given a most frosty reception. Questions flowed in staccato French. "Where was he? What are we to do? What's this about a grand house in Saint Omer? Is there a lady involved?"

This went on for five full minutes and I just stood and kept quiet. Suddenly she put her hands to her mouth "Vous et bande et blesse." You are bandaged and hurt. "Mon Dieu entre vitement s'il vous plait."

It was easy after that, Amelie just took over, unbandaged my bleeding wounds, dressed them with a soothing balm and then made me a warm coffee drink and gave me some meat and bread to eat all the while questioning me about Serge's activities and our various battles all of which she knew about through the messages passed down through friends and neighbours. Word always travelled quickly in the countryside as I well knew.

Slowly and haltingly, I explained as best I could the arrangement Serge and I had come to. He was now my official estate manager in France, we had agreed a wage and profit share and she was to be the occupier of a grand town house in Saint Omer if she chose to leave Gravelines.

Long into the evening we discussed all the ramifications of their future life, no more fishing or smuggling though and possibly the Customs men might be glad to see the back of a notorious reprobate. We talked on and then suddenly she said, "We go," in English, which truly surprised me. Two small and excited children were then told, in strict secrecy, just what was going to happen and their eyes lit up with excitement when they knew they would be with their father again.

Bed, a long rest and then breakfast next day gave me the energy for my next task, a trip to England and once I had explained my ideas about the herring boats, Amelie smiled and left the house without a word, returning ten minutes later with a typical French fisherman who I took a liking to immediately. In a short time I was to be crew that night when they left to go into the North Sea where they were certain Scottish or North of England herring boats would be encountered. A price was agreed.

After tearful hugs from Amelie and the children, I left, joined the fishing boat and we were away promptly with a favourable wind and out of the harbour to fairly calm seas.

CHAPTER 16
THE NORTH SEA

From 11pm to 6am we fished the waters of the north sea without any sign of a herring boat despite a very careful watch on the horizon. By morning, the wind rose, a heavy swell developed and we made a lot of water into the boat. I took my share of baling out despite the pains in my arms and legs. At about 7am, heavy rain fell and continued for the next two hours but the fishing improved so much that the skipper decided to stay out for a further four hours and reap the bounty of large cod and mackerel which were in abundance.

I helped as best I could until we had the small holds filled with fish and it was agreed that the warm weather despite the storms, would make the fish go off quickly and we turned for the French Coast to my dismay.

Then out of the pouring rain came a very small sailing trawler running fast under reduced sails. We hailed her loud and long and she finally turned into the wind and came alongside asking if we were in trouble. Reassuring him we were fine, I asked to speak to the Skipper and asked his possible destination. "Mind yer business," was gruffly spoken.

Shouting over the rising wind and heavy lashing waves I explained my need to reach a harbour in England and would pay for transport.

The Skipper roared with laughter at that, remarking, "I'm fleeing from a French Customs boat and you have delayed me long enough. Come aboard if you must but it's not something I would do in this weather."

I carried a lot of gold coin, both French and English in my money belt which I knew with a certainty would carry me straight to the bottom of the sea if I leapt on that heaving deck and missed my handhold. I realised the alternative was to remove the money belt, throw it aboard this small craft with a mean Skipper, and hope he didn't clear off before I could join him.

Yelling my intention, I asked him to bring his frail craft alongside the French vessel, threw my money belt over and then balanced precariously on the boat's gunwale and waited for the two boats rising and falling in the angry waves to coincide. That was a very hairy moment and waiting a long time, being constantly encouraged by all concerned I made the tremendous leap as the boats thrashed about. I landed half in and half out of the craft, feet trailing in the sea and my arms aching from the wounds that had now opened, blood flowing down my arm to the horror of the onlookers, but gritting my teeth I clung on and with extreme difficulty thrust first one leg, then the other over the thwart and I fell in an ignominious heap on to the deck.

On board the Kettle, for such was her name, I grabbed and painfully replaced my money belt, all the time under the very watchful eye of the Skipper.

"That was a very close shave, young man. You must be desperate to reach England. Are you on the run?"

Watching him carefully and letting him see my dirk in my boot when I pretended to check its safety, I retorted, "I'm paying you, I hope, a reasonable fee to get me to England providing I get there in one piece and until then I'm stuck with you and I am a smuggler and cattle drover also. What's this about French Customs?"

"You'll soon see, bonny lad," and at that moment a cannon shot landed just to the stern of our boat with a faint boom following shortly after.

"Stopping to pick you up has allowed these froggy bastards to catch me up. I was outsailing them easily until this!"

"Right, we're in this together," I said. "Where are the rest of the crew?"

"You're it, bonny lad, and while I have breath you will do exactly as I say and we might out run these thieving sods yet."

So started one of the most gruelling episodes of my short life. Waves hammered the boat and I was baling water, tightening sheets, making food, hauling sails as taut as I could. We beat as close as we possibly could to the wind and steered off the true wind and pointed successfully a good eight degrees closer than the French boat intent on overhauling us.

Zachary Clerk, the Skipper, certainly knew his boat and its capabilities. Three more shots were fired at us as the light faded but the cannon balls bounced harmlessly, well in our wake, and we continued our constant battle with the elements.

As the wind swung north westerly, we turned from our previous heading and sheeted hard with reduced sails we prepared for the long night ahead.

Zach was displaying signs of fatigue now and I suggested I take over the helm and he could take a few hours rest. He questioned my ability and fitness, looking hard at the blood on my leg but I assured him the bandage was secure and the bleeding had stopped.

After a furious debate, I was allowed to take the tiller and from the binnacle light was instructed to hold the present course of 338 degrees for three hours and then wake him as, by his reckoning, we were still only just off the distant Thames estuary.

For those three hours I remained as alert as I could. Waves crashed round us and the boat slewed in many different directions but always I returned to that 338 degrees heading. Pitch black night, alone on the cramped deck, Zach asleep under a meagre tarpaulin for cover, I questioned my wisdom in choosing this vessel.

Steadily we made progress through the waves, the reduced sail allowing a steady headway to be made without the boat constantly heeling and taking in water. Towards the end of that three long hours I realised this boat had good sea keeping qualities despite its appearance as a very small vessel.

I woke Zach with some reluctance. He was instantly alert, rose swiftly and checked the compass heading. That done, he looked long and hard at the sea state and heavy waves and announced, "We need to stay on this course till dawn and then we take a careful look at our surroundings because that Frenchy boat will still be around, I think, but may sheer off at dawn as we are near the English coast."

Dawn came with us both scanning the horizon which was clear from a first inspection but my eyes caught a glimpse of a yellowed sail far on the horizon and well astern. Zach reckoned the French were still in chase.

Hardening the sails and raising them fully again, we fairly flew through the water making, by his reckoning, about five knots and we stayed on this 335 degree course till noon.

Zach explained to me his intention now to change course to a heading of 310 degrees and we would run parallel to the coast hoping to outrun the French boat and this we did.

Thankfully the wind strayed to the south west and our progress, though slow, was steady at four to five knots I was told and twenty four hours of this activity brought Scarborough into view in the distance.

"Fancy landing in Scarborough, Jack, or go a little further?"

"Whitby might be better, Zach, as I can get a good horse from there and make for home."

My work and sleep on the boat with minimum food had sharpened me up nicely and both Zach and I had developed a high regard for one another.

Whitby Harbour saw me land, having paid Zach our agreed price.

Now for home.

Nobody took the slightest notice of my arrival. People went about their business as though this was a very normal happening and I suppose it was. As far as anybody could tell I was a sailor discharged from his boat and now looking for work.

Head down and moving quickly, I entered the town and found an ostlers where I purchased two good horses with saddles and made my way on the long journey to Brough.

CHAPTER 17
RETURN TO BROUGH

It's about eighty five miles from Whitby to Brough in Westmoreland and I travelled very carefully with my wounds. I arrived in my home area on the 8th September 1821.

Riding slowly now and leading my tired spare horse towards Ridley House, I noted the field we used as a stance full of good Scottish kylies, so a drove had stopped over for the night. A grey blur caught my eye and then Dag was next to my horse, wagging his tail and generally disturbing my nags. I dismounted and was fussed over greatly by the damned great beast. I walked the rest of the way to try and ease my tired bones, knowing full well that Giselle would scold me for fighting again.

What a sight! Running out of the house, skirts flying around her, my little Giselle leapt once again into my arms and we hugged and kissed for a lovely long time because I had missed her and my extended family very much and was so very relieved to be home.

More people came out as we neared the house, all smiling and Giles toddled, like his mother, straight into my arms for a big hug while my parents and others shook my hand and bade me a welcome home.

Sitting round the table after a late dinner, I recounted most of my adventures to the party at the table and was questioned closely about Giselle's parents' graves and location. With that explained and a brief talk about the property arrangements, I was very thankful to go to bed feeling that I had accomplished something significant as I said to Giselle. But once together in bed, she questioned me very closely about the fight I had survived in Saint Omer, as I knew she would and whilst she entirely understood my motives and deep anger at her personal treatment, she gave me a good 'telling off' that I had anticipated.

Goodness knows how I was to survive in this lawless age without occasional recourse to violence but that was not a subject I thought it wise to pursue and we eventually settled for a long loving embrace.

Next morning I silently crossed off the upstart bastard who had caused such grief to Giselle and that left me two more people I needed to deal with: that bloody magistrate Cedric P. Cleasby who had arranged for Giselle's abduction so long ago and Silas Kirk who I feared most after his threat to our son.

George Cook had written from Bilsdale whilst I was in France. He would like to visit soon as he was on a drove from Scotland and hoped to be in the area shortly. Reading his letter it seemed he was keeping out of the clutches of two robust and solid young ladies who seemed to have their hearts set on marrying him, when they were not fighting each other! I looked forward very much to seeing him again, he was a dear friend and had shown himself as a true and loyal ally in our adventures travelling to Suffolk last year.

That morning after my check on my own cattle and the drovers' beasts, I caught up with Josh Liddell and his two boys. We walked across to the farm I had purchased, Bank Side Farm, and viewed with great delight the channels that had been dug to divert the stream and water the whole area. It was in its infancy as a project but already I could see the way in which Josh had set to and the benefits would be soon evident, which I commented on. Josh reckoned he had kept both his sons usefully employed but the amount of food they were consuming had him gravely concerned. I said I would resolve that by paying them for each hour they worked for me on this project.

James' two sheep had lambed successfully but he had lost one of the four that were born, however he had bought for pennies in the market two orphaned lambs which he hand reared also and they were all looking fit and well. That lad had potential because I had only bought him two sheep in lamb but he now had seven in hand, a very capable young man, I suspected.

I suggested to Josh that I would like him to accompany me to Carlisle and explained about the huge mad bull I had purchased in late May this year and I wondered if he could work his magic on it. We discussed timings because further trips were being frowned on by Giselle but I was determined to show that bull and win a major prize.

CHAPTER 18
TO CARLISLE

Two days after arriving home, being properly bandaged, we set off in grand style for Carlisle. I drove in my two horse carriage and Josh was in charge as we rode. I was dressed as a country Squire now and after an overnight stop in Penrith, we made our way to John Fisher's farm on the outskirts of the city where I had left my wild bull, to we make ourselves known. Or we tried to.

John Fisher, the farmer drover, looked very hard at the smart carriage and me before the connection dawned on him. We shook hands warmly and I introduced Josh Liddell without letting on just what his position was with me as we went to look at this mad bull which we could hear roaring as we neared its quarters.

As we walked, John confessed it had cost him far more than he anticipated to keep the bull, primarily it was wages for men to constantly oversee the mad beast. I suggested I would not be afraid to discuss some costs with him.

He asked what I intended to do with 'Hector' as they had christened him so I mentioned I intended to put him in Carlisle Show next week and he laughed fit to burst.

"That damned great thing would absolutely wreck any show you put him in. He wants putting down if you ask me," he retorted once he ceased laughing.

I took no notice, winked at a worried-looking Josh and we wandered over to the bull's pen. The noise inside was fearsome, crashing hooves, raucous bellowing and three very scared men outside with long poles and with hooks on to try and control Hector and help him get some exercise but his nose was bleeding slightly.

Truly he looked magnificent, pawing the ground and giving raucous bellows such that John and his men stepped back at one particular lunge but at that moment Josh began to talk and hum and it was a sight to behold again.

Slowly, very slowly, the huge bull became aware of this strange noise emanating from Josh Liddell. He still paced about his stall but was occasionally stopping and watching before cavorting off again. This continued for ten minutes or so to the amazement of all those standing nervously near.

Gradually Hector succumbed to the gentle noise, ceased his mad charges at the door to his byre, stared straight at Josh and then walked meekly over and allowed Josh to stroke his broad flanks.

Utter and complete silence followed this demonstration and Josh was getting almost reverent looks from John and his men such that they stepped back completely bewildered when Josh led Hector out of the byre and calmly walked him into the nearby field where he commenced grazing but always kept an eye on Josh, listening to his gentle words and sing song voice.

We left Josh and Hector communing with each other and wandered over to John's house for tea. There I agreed to reimburse him for his extra expenses and he was very relieved. Then we discussed my plans. I was determined to enter Hector into Carlisle Show which was held traditionally on the 19th September for cattle. Josh would remain with the bull until and after the show but my sole purpose in all this business was to get Mr C. P. Cleasby sufficiently interested to buy the beast and then I explained why.

John and his men were aghast at the sheer effrontery of Cleasby to pretend to great deeds as a Magistrate, to purport to be a national expert on cattle and particularly bulls and then have young maidens kidnapped for him to deflower. After that exposure I had many willing helpers.

CHAPTER 19
BULL HECTOR TO CARLISLE SHOW

It was now the 10th September and Carlisle Show was on the 19th so I had a lot of planning and skulduggery to attend to and I was not sure if Josh Liddell was up to it. Nothing ventured, he was my employee but I did not want him to have brushes with the law against his better judgement.

Taking him aside, we sat in John Fisher's farmhouse with the door firmly locked and I gave him the outline of my plan and his mounting grin and occasional rubbing of his hands gave me the distinct impression that away from female influences, here was a man somewhat in my own mould, a daredevil willing to take a chance and able to give a good account of himself. I must admit that in the days he had been in my employ he had broadened out in the chest and seemed if anything a little taller now with good food in him.

All was agreed between us and I set off next day to the city of Carlisle to find a silversmith's shop which I had been advised was near to Carlisle Castle. Leaving my horse at a nearby ostlers, I walked through and found the shop which was dismal, run down looking and generally scruffy, probably just what I was looking for. Peering through the dusty window, there were a lot of poor looking bits and pieces but to my surprise a largish silver plate with some very small writing in the very centre. Could this be what I wanted?

Stooping a little, I entered the low doorway and stood in a veritable shambles of a shop. Parcels on the floor, cats sprawling everywhere and a counter piled high with candlesticks, empty boxes, chains of silver appearing links and the scruffiest bespectacled man you have ever seen.

His greeting was unusual. "Piss off!" He waved a heavy cane at me threateningly but I just seized it and pulled him towards me. Bless me but he stank!

"What a wonderful greeting you gave me and I am not surprised you seem to have little trade. Shall I piss off then or would you like to discuss some business with me, you bad tempered scoundrel?"

Everything went still for a while, even the cats stopped wowling. "Just what do you think you want in my shop, Sir? Have you come to rob me as well?"

Slowly I explained that I had in mind to make a particular purchase. Namely a real silver plate not dissimilar to that shown in his window. He put his hand to his head and sat wearily on a stool behind the counter. He was unmoving and silent for so long that I thought he had taken a bad turn but he was just collecting his thoughts.

That morning, he said, his landlord had appeared

and as landlords do, demanded his rent but the recent disturbances which I had heard about had stopped his already poor trade and he was selling as much as he could to cover his rent. But had nothing for the landlord who was expected back at any moment.

I asked him to bring out from the window the silver plate I had seen as I wished to examine it and on having it handed to me saw, from the reverse, that it was hallmarked silver but I was unsure of the next marking which he explained, "That's the castle mark to show the goods emanated from Newcastle-upon-Tyne."

All well and good. Next I looked very carefully at the small inscription in the plate centre which although almost illegible said 'K. Jones, Winner 1810' but had been barely scratched almost in an amateur hand.

Now to business. "My name is not important to you, you may call me 'Sir' and I believe from the shop front that you may be Mr Algernon, is that so?"

"Correct, Sir, and do you wish to buy this plate by any chance?"

"I certainly do and wish to know how much you will charge to both sell the plate, remove the present engraving which is a very shallow cut and the inscribe it 'Carlisle Show 1821. Best Galloway Bull in Show'."

"£6.10s.0d would be the amount I would want from you in cash and I would want a further 10 shillings to remove the present shallow engraving and put in the letters you suggest."

Closely examining the plate, its outer rim was adorned

with pressed images of leaves and flowers almost representing a laurel wreath which suited me fine.

"£6.10s.0d is what I will pay you in cash once the work is completed and I must tell you I will be here at 10am tomorrow to collect it, complete. Do you understand and do we have a deal?"

Scratching his miserably skinny chin, he eventually said, "Yes, we have a deal, cash on collection but I would like a deposit please in case my landlord returns."

I left the shop with a receipt for my £2.0s.0d deposit safely stored in my money belt around my waist.

Next I went looking for the printers of pamphlets as these and the newspapers had become very popular for passing local information on very quickly. Printed on cheap paper and distributed free by paid urchins to passersby they gave instant news to the literate and were read out in taverns to those who could not read or write, of which there were many at that time.

At the printers I described the details I wished to see on my free sheet which stated that:

'A Wonderful Silver Plate, suitably inscribed, will be presented to the winner of the 'Best Galloway Bull' at next week's Carlisle Show. All are welcome with entries being taken on the day.

It is hoped that a well known local magistrate, renowned throughout the region for his knowledge of cattle, will be attending.'

The printer assured me, for a fee, that the same detail would appear in the next issue of the 'Gazette'. I paid his invoice suggesting he made the receipt out to 'Mr Silas Kirk Esq'.

Back then to John Fisher's farm where he had offered Josh and I accommodation, for a fee, which I was glad to pay.

In the yard, Hector the bull was behaving as would a normal bull in his prime, roaring at nearby cows, tossing his head, prancing about but strangely fascinated and attached to Josh Liddell who the farm hands had dubbed the 'Bull Singer' which he thought most amusing.

Days were spent washing, grooming with difficulty, cutting hair, plaiting the tail and generally smartening the mad bull Hector into a really fine animal for presentation. Nothing was left to chance, he was fed regularly, walked frequently to retain his magnificent muscled structure, sung to by Josh and looked the very part of a Prize Winning Bull, or so I hoped.

Word had quickly spread about the forthcoming Silver Plate Prize and there were far more entries than I personally expected. Visiting my silversmith to pay the balance of money and collect my plate, I made it very clear to Mr Algernon that I was sure he suspected this was one of the plates stolen from him recently if he was ever questioned. Further he could now destroy in front of me any receipts and journal entries and I left with the distinct impression he knew exactly what I was driving at.

Came the day of Carlisle Show and despite a steady breeze the weather held. Crowds thronged the road and spread widely across the field. Tents displaying goods made locally were erected and the tinkers and panniermen had gathered to display and sell their pans, pegs, pots, knives, forks, stools. All the items to attract housewives and husbands to haggle and buy. Children flocked around running and shouting with sheer enjoyment so it was a very happy atmosphere over the whole field.

Set back behind wattle fencing were cows, sheep, pigs, goats, rabbits, hens and with pride of place a separate area for the judging of these entrants. Officious top hatted local luminaries were noisily judging various classes.

Hector's arrival, with Josh leading him, brought a hush to proceedings as word had it that he was a very mad bull, fearsome if roused and dangerous to be near and for this reason he was given a wide berth through the crowd but with Josh quietly humming he only pranced about a little. Generally showing off but under complete control, he certainly looked the part as he strolled along to his allotted place in the large bull ring, not failing to bellow a challenge to all about him.

This sound drew the attention of the judges who looked fearfully in his direction but seemed reassured when they noted his acceptance of Josh's guiding hand and willingness to be tethered without too much fuss. Other bulls in the competition, far more than anticipated, all seemed somehow much smaller by comparison but I only saw all this from a suitable distance. I had borrowed some drover's clothing from John Fisher and some of his men and I hoped I could remain unrecognised in view of what I hoped was about to happen.

"There's yon daft bugger, Cleasby," I heard a bystander remark and noting the direction of his glance I spotted the bastard I had made all these complicated arrangements for. So far so good.

John Fisher had agreed that he acted as the bull's keeper for a distant owner who he did not really know. All negotiations, he said, had been carried out with an agent in France by post once the animal arrived at his farm. But he was to make it clear that the agent had insisted the bull would be for sale to the highest bidder after the competition was over. He would receive any offers.

Cleasby was spotted talking to the judges and looking frequently at Hector so the plot went forward.

Slowly the time dragged round until the final event of the day. The judging for the Silver Plate to be awarded to the best Galloway Bull on show. Gathering together the judges slowly made their way around the beasts and when they had carried out a close examination, they asked that each animal trot round the outside of the ring to display its musculature. All went well and six of the eight bulls entered behaved impeccably, walked sedately round the ring edge and returned to their allotted space, but of course one frisky young bull would stop and bellow at Hector, challenging him in no uncertain terms. Naturally our big stupid bugger fell for it, reared right up on his hind legs and would have landed on top of the now cowering challenger had not Josh stepped in and actually shouted at Hector, "Down!"

Damn me he did just that, came down, snorted almost flame. The challenger backed off rapidly and our boy came to rest, pawing the ground but appearing happy he had 'won' that encounter.

Cleasby, looking on and watching this reaction, actually walked over in his domineering way and spoke briefly to Josh before looking most annoyed that the judges told him to "Clear Off".

At his turn to parade, Hector shone like a light. Walking with a jaunty step, he looked every inch the perfect bull and in fact many in the crowd cheered as he went past which was very unusual.

He was last but one. The final bull was displayed but failed to make any impression on the crowd and hopefully the judges.

At these events three animals are selected from the bunch and placed separately when they are revisited by the judges and the selection commences with the Third Prize, if there is one, going to the first selected and it wasn't Hector, then after great deliberation a second animal was chosen and because it wasn't Hector, we all realised he was the winner of the Silver Plate which John Fisher was delighted to collect.

Once the Plate was in his hands and the cheering died down, John was taken to one side by Cleasby and questioned about the bull and its price. I'd told John to play this along slowly, not so much to tease a good price out of the swine of a man, but to encourage him to approach the bull, in Josh's presence and feel he had the control over the animal that he widely claimed to possess.

Laboriously slowly the negotiations went on, a good

price, in fact a stunning profit, was offered but John insisted that the bull was notoriously dangerous and was Mr Cleasby entirely satisfied that he could control the animal when it was in his possession. I heard all this discussion from a small distance and so, deliberately on my part, did a whole lot of other people who suffered Cleasby's loud remonstration that "I know all about bulls and wild animals and of course I know what I am doing my man! Sell me the animal immediately for the £50.0s.0d I have offered and be done with you."

With a bowed head John agreed to the deal, shook hands and collected the money immediately. A grinning Cleasby, a triumphant smile on his face was about to leave when John suggested that as part of the agreement, Josh would walk the Bull Hector to Cleasby's farm some ten miles distant and this generous offer was accepted.

With a grand sweep of his top hat to the crowd and a second one to the judges, Cleasby went to his carriage and was whisked away in a swirl of dust.

Waking next morning and preparing for the journey home, I welcomed Josh who had returned footsore and tired much later the previous night and had taken the opportunity for a short sleep in before he, like me, enjoyed a substantial breakfast.

I had given a lot of thought to how to proceed and decided to give £20.0s.0d to both John Fisher and Josh Liddell for a job very well done which they were overjoyed to accept.

Two days later a hired ostler guided our two horses and

our carriage into the grounds of Ridley House and after the usual boisterous greeting, we all fled inside for tea and a catch up on local gossip.

Days later came the shocking news that a prominent magistrate in the area and a well known expert on cattle, had been gored to death by his recently purchased bull. We heard this news and we looked suitably contrite in front of the rest of the gathered people but once alone Giselle suggested that I may have had a hand in the demise of this rotten dirty womanising man. I then told her the full story of how I had learned of Cleasby's whereabouts and his proud boast that 'He knew cattle and bulls in particular'.

I then had to confess that I had very carefully engineered the whole episode from start to finish, buying the bull, realising that in Josh I had the perfect person to calm the crazy animal. I then created the 'Silver Plate' as a prize and once the bull won the Show, as I hoped, Cleasby couldn't wait to get his hands on it and it proved his demise.

Giselle took this news in a most calm and ladylike way, a brief touch of her handkerchief to her eyes and then composed herself, made the sign of the cross and exclaimed, "Jack, that was very dangerous for you both but thank you from the bottom of my heart. He seems to have been a particularly evil man."

Hector, for all his ravings and savagery, had been an absolutely magnificent animal with the potential to be a very valuable bull to be offered for stud.

Josh and I had schemed a little. We both knew nobody

could get near enough to despatch him which is why, once I had the news of Cleasby's demise, I sent Josh over to calm the bull down and negotiate his purchase. He was the only known person who could exert any control over Hector and through the good offices of John Fisher we bought the wild bull from Cleasby's estate and expected it to be arriving in the next few weeks. Then it could be offered to the highest bidder for its progeny. Josh would remain in charge and bring him to Brough once the sale was completed.

CHAPTER 20
CUSTOMS AND EXCISE

Customs and Excise rode up the long driveway the next day, recognisable by their distinct uniforms and brass buttons. We had met previously when they accused me of harbouring tobacco and tea but I was then without any of the goods on me and when they tried to rough me up it became somewhat fierce and they left a little worse for wear.

This being a Sunday, most of the family, friends and servants had gone to church and would not be back till after midday but I had instructions to put a large piece of beef in the oven and make sure the fire did not die down. I'd done all this and was outside busying myself when Dag's low growl warned me we had company.

These two could only mean trouble in either the long or short term. I had no contraband in the house or in any of my hiding places but that might not stop my past misdemeanours catching up with me.

Unwilling to invite them indoors I upended a nearby log and sat to await their arrival and the reason for their coming all the way from Carlisle.

Approaching warily, one eye on me and one on my dog, they suggested, "You are being investigated for the smuggling of large quantities of tea and tobacco and we wish to take a statement from you."

In other words they were on a 'fishing trip'. I smiled and said nothing.

"Rutherford, are you listening to me?" said the elder of the two, but again I kept quiet.

"Rutherford, we know you have been smuggling tea and tobacco from a very reliable source, now come clean and tell us all you know and we may be lenient."

I stood slowly and walked in a very deliberate way right up close to the speaker and whispered quietly, "It's 'Sir' to you when you address me and please remember, you are on my private land without authority or any search warrant so I suggest you turn around and quickly walk away, because it would give the greatest pleasure to throw you out by the scruff of the neck. Come back with some evidence of my alleged misdemeanours and make sure you get permission before you enter."

Without another word they mounted their horses and rode away, raising dust from the road in their hurry to depart.

Mulling over that meeting, it would appear somebody had spoken out of turn about my exploits. Could this be the influence of Silas Kirk in his bid to do me down?

Pondering this and many other possible reasons for that visit, I resolved on Monday to visit Brough and Kirkby Stephen and leave a message with the usual sources for Reuben Connor to make contact very quickly. I would ensure from a careful watch that I was not being followed.

But that day, when the church party returned, I drew Giselle to one side and brought her up to date with this new twist of fate and while she gasped and muttered, "How terrible," I played it down to ease her worries.

Monday saw me make my visits and the rest of the week passed uneventfully until Friday saw the familiar figure of Reuben and his irascible donkeys trudging up the drive to my house where we met, shook hands, then wandered into a nearby barn after he secured his animals.

"So what's all this about then, Jack? Messages from two people to contact you urgently so it had better be good. I'm losing money just standing talking to you." He was always gentle with words but after I accidentally stood on his foot he ceased wowling after a while and discussed the situation we both had a keen interest in.

It became very clear after long intense discussion that our activities, known to very few people, had been given to the Revenue as a tip off for them to act on. Strangely, it was the tea they were taking the most interest in and on that subject Reuben produced my quarterly delivery from Mrs Clark in Liverpool together with a receipted invoice which I tucked into my money belt.

Given the number of enemies Reuben had, he lived in constant danger of being arrested, as did I, and we agreed to keep in very close touch with each other to anticipate just what was going on particularly after my dismissal, some time ago, of Albert Atkins and I told Reuben the sorry tale of him succumbing to drunkenness.

Sure enough he knew all about the matter and brought me up to date on some disturbing developments, that Atkins had been seen in the area with none other than Silas Kirk who had a young lady with him at all times but she always had a heavy shawl over most of her features.

Silas Kirk in the area could only mean serious trouble and the fact he was dragging round another possibly foreign young lady gave me food for thought. I wondered if by any chance it might be the young lady I had seen in St Omer.

Once I had matters on the farm moving to my satisfaction, I left Giselle in charge and took the long road to Carlisle to look at some more cattle but also to enquire of my many contacts, including Reuben's friends, if Silas Kirk was in the area.

CHAPTER 21
CARLISLE

Steady riding on my excellent horse saw Carlisle appear in the early Autumn morn and I found some accommodation, stabled my horse and started out for the Cattle Market. I always carry money in the form of gold coin in a stout belt with suitable pouches firmly fastened to my waist with a large buckle. Just by approaching and looking at the gathered herds of cattle I was marked out to the villains as a likely target for robbery but the reputation I have for fierce battle and the very large Irish wolfhound at my side usually avoided any problems.

But unknown to me and before I could meet any friends for information, I found I was being followed very carefully round the mart by four likely robbers who looked as though they both meant business and could take care of themselves. Dag knew they were there. He had growled deep in his throat when one man came close and he had his watchful eye on them. For my part I carried my drover's forked stick as usual but that was useless in a scrap and I would rely, as always on the long sharp dirk I kept in the top of my boot.

It's always the same at these country marts, some swaggering men become convinced they can get rich very quickly with bluster and loud words. Not these four, they went about their task in a very thorough and organised way and I was having to concentrate very hard on the best way to outwit them. Ideally I wanted a narrow vennel or passageway with no exit, that way I could tackle them head on but at the most two at a time and of course my dog couldn't wait to draw blood in a fight standing by my side.

Something about the demeanour of these men was familiar to me and it occurred to me that I was possibly dealing with former soldiers turned mercenaries and that could bode ill for me.

I was familiar with many parts of Carlisle and my recent purchase from the silversmith brought to mind the narrow entrance to his shop and its permanently locked state. That could be the place to do battle.

To lull my adversaries into a false sense of security I looked carefully at their physique, realised two of them were overweight and walking heavily, then I broke into a frightened looking run, looking over my shoulder all the time and causing my dog a great amount of puzzlement. We normally stand and fight. The odds were not in our favour yet but that might soon change.

On and on I ran, the villains following and I dodged through small alleyways always making good progress to reach my chosen killing ground which I found after ten minutes of hard running. Sure enough, in the narrow alley the door to the silversmiths was firmly locked and a sign stated 'Closed'. All good.

First on the scene was the largest and apparently fittest of the thieves who charged into the alley with a drawn sword only to be tripped up by Dag to fall at my feet. I laid him out with some heavy blows, stamped on his arm and broke it, then leapt back as the second man appeared, again with a drawn sword but on seeing his companion's fate he paused briefly, at which Dag was at his throat and his death scream was terrifying to hear. Well it certainly unnerved the next man who had stopped just in the start of the alley but I leapt over writhing man and dog and ran the man through on his upper leg with my long dirk and he dropped bleeding to the ground.

Next came the slowest of the thieves, a plump, crafty eyed man. He weighed up the situation in a second and turned to run, but Dag had him by the leg. He fell heavily and it was all I could do in a short time to prevent Dag tearing out his throat.

All done with little damage to me but that would not always be the case. Using their clothing, I bound their hands and feet firmly, staunched some of the copious flow of blood and decided to ask a few questions of these men.

It took all of an hour to gain the truth and some more arms seemed to get broken in the confusion of questioning but eventually it came out. Yes, they were all former soldiers, recruited in Manchester by a Mr Kirk who would pay handsomely for my capture and delivery to him in any state.

Men had been despatched by Kirk to Dumfries and Penrith Markets with the same instructions and I wondered just where he was getting all this money from. I knew magistrate Cleasby was no longer on the scene and could only assume he had taken a substantial deposit of the procurement of another young lady for a 'virgin bride'.

Whilst all this was happening some urchins had appeared and following them some local housewives who stared in horror at the carnage we had wrought and were all for having me arrested but I was able to explain my presence. When an Officer of the Law appeared, he thanked me for my brave act as a decent citizen and confirmed he had watched these men for many days as they jostled people in the mart and stole from them. It was his pleasure to arrange to have them taken to gaol and made a written statement explaining just what had happened and the consequences of the savage attack made by four men against a simple drover and his dog. The Officer reckoned my statement would be sufficient to keep them inside until the next Assizes which would be in the New Year. They could stay longer for me!

Once back at the Cattle Mart all trading had ceased. Men were shovelling ordure into carts and generally tidying up as I arrived. Nothing further could be gained from staying and I made my way to the ostlers to collect my horse and head carefully and warily for home.

My senses were fully alert now to any perceived danger and when a very smelly, shifty looking man came sidling up, Dag growled and I loosened my dirk but the man stopped short of my position, looked me firmly in the eye and stated, "Do you know Reuben Connor the packman?"

I gave him a positive reply.

He took a clay pipe from his pocket and slowly brought it to light with a few quick puffs. "He said if I found you, to check you were Jack Rutherford and be very careful how I approached you, which I've done. I'm to tell you a Silas Kirk has been seen on the northern edge of the town with two big blokes and a slip of a young girl. He said you might pay me for my trouble."

Giving him a few pence I collected my horse and set off on the long trek home with a hell of a lot of thinking to do. I was getting closer. The sooner I caught up with Kirk and dealt with him the happier my life would be and I would now leave no stone unturned to find him.

CHAPTER 22
TEA SOIREE, ARREST!

Eventually Dag and I returned to Ridley House and after some fond greetings and hugs for my son Giles, I went about my daily business watching the cattle droves come and go, arranging the gathering of my animals for sale to the butchers and all the household tasks that now took over my next few days.

It was now late September, the nights were drawing in a little and we had recovered sufficient harvest of barley, hay and had a good field of turnips to see us over the coming winter.

Wednesday that week, Giselle called me and made me sit and listen to her. Big surprise. She was organising an end of season 'Tea Soiree' here at Ridley Hall and all the great and the good of the area had been invited and had accepted. My role was to keep out of the way apparently. I was to visit Kirkby Stephen at once and buy some smart up to date men's wear in keeping with my newfound status and not wear the drovers' clothes that I usually favoured and that was that!

Visiting the fancy clothing shop did not appeal at all

but once there I was agreeably surprised at the quality of the clothing available and chose, with Giselle's help, a very smart outfit that made even me look prosperous. So once home I pranced about our bedroom in this remarkable outfit and had Giselle in peals of laughter at my antics, doffing my hat and doing the bended knee thing.

Came the day of the Soiree the weather was blissful, occasional white clouds but a remarkably warm sunny day and the crowds came in great number from some long distances. I arranged for James and Theodore Liddell to control the field where the various horses and carriages would be placed while their owners enjoyed tea and cakes in the French style that Giselle had created.

It all seemed a little bit fussy to me but society locally were entranced by this breath of continental flair suddenly thrust in their midst and Giselle certainly made sure they paid handsomely for the privilege. They say money attracts more money and I could quite see just where that saying came from. Our bank balance was very healthy.

Cakes and tea flowed freely and many local dandies and their spouses soaked up the atmosphere. Giselle had even found a small three piece band to play a little light music. She suggested the attendees attempted the 'Gavotte'. The band played and she demonstrated the steps which quickly found favour with the ladies and slowly all their partners. It was a very busy drawing room that lovely evening and it remains very clear in my memory…

Not for the dance, or the company or Giselle's smiling

face as we danced together but for those bastard Customs and Revenue men who crashed on to the floor, arrested me and put me in irons and dragged me away to gaol in Brough for smuggling.

My embarrassment was complete, the music stopped abruptly, all eyes turned upon me and Giselle broke down in tears at both my arrest and the ignominy of the whole situation.

Thrusting through the crowds, with my hands manacled together, I was unceremoniously plonked on a horse and the Customs men, all twelve of them, escorted me down to Brough, unknown to them but followed by my big wolfhound until I told him to go home.

Relief showed on some of the faces of my captors at this. I maintained a silence, determined to give nothing away until I saw the evidence for my arrest.

Silently we wound our way into town and I was placed, once again, in the gaol as had happened some years ago when I wrecked the local market.

None of my gaolers were known to me and must have been brought in especially from Carlisle or Penrith but once they started to converse I would get some idea of their background.

No paperwork had been produced at the time of my arrest and sure enough magistrate and friend Jeremiah Ridley was heard to arrive in the building and demand my immediate release but this was refused as a warrant for my arrest for smuggling tea had been sworn the previous week in Carlisle on information received from a reliable source. I could guess who that was, bloody Kirk. I kept my counsel.

Seeing the warrant, Jeremiah left but not before warning the Revenue men they had better tread very carefully in this matter.

But what did the warrant say? I refused to speak to any of my captors despite numerous attempts at conversation and I restricted myself to thanking whoever brought my water and poor food.

Two full days I remained in that cell until an officious looking clerk appeared and announced, "We have reason to believe that you have taken delivery of a quantity of illegal tea recently and we intend to prosecute you with the full powers of the law for this illegal activity."

So that's how it was. The man cleared off when I refused to speak to him for an hour and that gave me time to think.

That bloody Albert Atkins, acting as my manager, had seen Reuben Connor bring me the tea but was unaware that it had been paid for. I remembered I had put the receipt in my money belt for safe keeping.

Escape seemed impossible but I had been in worse situations than this, but not a lot worse and I racked my brain for a solution.

My prison comprised a single storey stone built former dwelling house, commandeered some time ago by the Town Council and used as a holding cell for arrested people awaiting transport to Penrith or Carlisle for a court hearing. In my youth I had been locked up in this building after an incident with pigs in the market place so I was familiar, as a local, with its background.

Bars covered the window to my cell and there was only the one entrance which was firmly locked at all times. Any other way out? What about the roof and what could I do to reach that height and get away?

But to what avail? I would then be a fugitive from justice, hunted down constantly and that would play right in to the hands of Silas Kirk who I was convinced was behind all this.

Supposing I could get out, then what? The simple answer was to get home, grab my money belt and the formal receipt and get back in to gaol before I was missed. Could it be done?

Better to have tried and failed, so I broke my vow of silence and asked if I could have a chair to sit on and a wooden form to sleep on rather than the floor. Much muttering and cursing came from the other side of the door but an hour later it opened, my food was delivered together with a chair, two logs and a broad board to sleep on, then I was locked in. I reckoned it to be just dark outside so that would be about 8pm and I was not normally checked or bothered by my gaolers until the next morning bringing water to wash and some food.

Ignoring the chair I placed the long 6ft board at an angle to the wall and after some slow attempts managed to reach the first of the roof tiles with my hands and damn it they were firmly fastened.

I moved that board very quietly right round that

damned dark room, listening all the time for the return of the guard who twice listened outside my door and then retreated.

Eventually, in one corner, I found loose tiles that I silently removed creating a sufficient space for me to haul my body up and on to the roof where I could just discern the rear of the building against the darkening sky. Voices below and I froze until they moved away and I could smell tobacco smoke in the air. Men enjoying a late pipe before returning to watch duties.

Slowly, ever so slowly, I waited till their movements faded then I crept along the roof to the adjoining building and moved across that roof to complete my escape by shinning down a metal pipe to the ground. I paused now and took my bearings because for this to work I had to come back to this precise point and re-enter my cell without being found out.

It was cold now but I had suffered much greater cold on the roads so I dodged from building to building and made my way out of Brough and headed for my home where I would be a most surprising visitor.

Quickly covering the groun,d I reached Ridley House and knocked very hard on the front door which was eventually opened by my father holding a damn great cudgel which he raised to flatten me until he realised who it was and let me in with a gasp of surprise. Dag appeared and made a fuss then went back to his kennel. Silently then I mounted the stairs to our bedroom and I took the precaution to knock gently three times before I opened the bedroom door to a very surprised Giselle.

It was some moments before she released me from her arms and then I explained my mission which she immediately understood. We found my money belt where I had left it, extracted the receipt and then whispering my love for her I met my father who swore he had seen nothing. A big wink and then I was back to Brough.

It was very dark by now but my night vision was excellent and I knew the area very well so within the hour I was back outside my departure point and no sign of alarm. So far so good.

Now I had to climb the water pipe that to my dismay seemed very loosely connected to the building but I had to get back onto that roof to go across two more roofs to reach my own cell roof.

Fortunately I am strongly built without being too heavy and with great care I pulled myself up using footholds to minimise my weight on the pipe. Gradually I gained the roof. To my mind I had made enough noise to wake the dead but it must have been my heightened senses, as nothing moved in the area. Careful to move as quietly as possible, I located the right roof, found my escape hole and lowered myself slowly on to my long board and replaced the tiles as best I could. With luck I would be out of this place in twelve hours.

Placing the useful board on the two logs I was able to make a bed off the floor and slept well, in fact so well that the gaolers had to wake me up to give me water to wash, food and a warm drink, for which I thanked them. Then I learned that the Justice was coming that morning to arraign me for trial and I had best be well behaved.

Duly at ten o'clock the Judge could be heard arriving and from the noise a large crowd had gathered outside.

Handcuffed again I was thrust into the room where the Judge, a youngish man without his customary wig and cloak, looked at me over his glasses and asked if I had anything to say.

"I believe I have been arrested for an alleged offence of smuggling tea into my house recently. Is this correct?"

The Judge looked at the warrant in front of him, studied it for quite a while and then remarked, "That is perfectly correct. You are accused of taking a delivery of contraband tea from a well known person adept at avoiding the Customs and Excise Officers. What have you to say, Sir?"

"In front of these witnesses I would like you to delve into my jacket where you will find a piece of paper which will throw a very different light on these matters," I said.

"This is entirely out of order, Sir. To what do you refer?"

"A signed receipt for the tea I bought from Liverpool is in my pocket and I wish you and only you to remove it and confirm it is genuine."

Without more ado the Judge rose, asked me to raise my hands, searched in my pocket and produced the receipt from Mrs Clark.

Returning to his table, he very, very carefully read the

document, turned it over twice, read it again and threw his hands in the air.

"Never have I known such witless goings on as this case. Why on earth did the Officers not search you and produce the evidence of your innocence?"

It was not for me to comment but I reckoned that if that receipt had indeed been in my pocket it would never have seen that light of day again if the Revenue had found it. I kept my mouth shut once again.

"Release that man immediately please and ask him to join me at this table. Fetch all the Customs and Excise officers into this room now."

I have never seen such dejected creatures as those Revenue Officers when that Judge had finished with them. He had a command of the English language that tore them apart as if they had been flayed.

I had the distinct impression that heads would roll after this event and I had a warm feeling of joy when it was suggested I would receive a written letter of apology which would be printed in the local newspaper.

CHAPTER 23
GEORGE COOK ARRIVES

Walking home to Ridley House from my incarceration I gave very serious thought to the vengeful antics of Silas Kirk. I had heard of him in Carlisle on my recent trip and his presence in the area caused me great misgivings. One thing was certain and that was that he would strike again as soon as the opportunity presented itself. I could not go on the attack, as all my instincts cried out to do, until it was clear just where he was to be found. He was a cunning devil, deliberately preying on me and trying to make me feel insecure and vulnerable.

Once home and all the hundreds of questions answered, Giselle announced that George Cook had arrived that morning, exhausted from a long hard ride from Scotland and had been unceremoniously packed off to bed to rest, reassured that I was likely to be home that very day.

Estate matters filled my time with orders for fodder, sale of winter cattle in Carlisle Mart and arranging for their transport by drove before the bad weather set in. Funnily enough, despite many enquiries being placed around the area, there were no reliable drovers to be found as they were all on the big movements of cattle to the distant voracious markets of southern England. A so called Industrial Revolution was being mentioned in the newspapers where steam power was driving massive cotton mills and changing cities into filthy places that nevertheless provided a steady income to those who could work. Meat was the luxury food they insisted on buying, thank goodness, and cattle prices had risen to very good levels.

It was with this in mind that I was anxious to release some of my own herd to give a nice income but there were no drovers. Giselle would go mad if I took them and I pondered long and hard on this when there was a commotion at my office door. In walked a grinning George Cook who shook me warmly by the hand despite, as he said, "I am mixing with common criminals and ne'er do wells now."

A pretend clout to his face put paid to that and we embraced as good friends and continued our banter over a glass of wine.

George had 'escaped' the clutches of two or three young ladies of his home, Chop Gate in Bilsdale, North Yorkshire, by making a rapid retreat on foot to Falkirk where he had found good work as a very experienced drover, taking a huge herd of beast down to Carlisle Mart where they had been sold for a very handsome profit. He had immediately retraced his steps to Falkirk, this time on horseback and had paid all his Letters of Credit to the entire satisfaction of the Scottish dealers and had then commenced the journey to see me. In Penrith he heard the rumours that I had been arrested by the Revenue and resolved to come to my aid as quickly as possible but his horse went lame outside Appleby, was given to the ostler to recover, so he set out to walk as fast as he could to my aid.

That explained his deep weariness and lack of sleep and though I was very touched by this loyal friendship, I played it down a little by suggesting his only motive was to keep out of the clutches of the Bilsdale ladies.

"You just cannot believe the lengths those young ladies will go to to try and snare a man who doesn't want snaring," he said. "And fight! They battle among themselves, yelling and shouting when they think I cannot hear and then simper and throw coy glances at me when I appear. Jack, it's more than a man can stand. I've no intention of marrying and want to remain a free man to do as I please."

Big words from a bloke who I know Giselle thinks very highly of and indeed she has remarked to me many times that George would be a man who would settle down nicely with the right girl.

So we talked on for an hour or so, had a meal and then I stated I had some urgent business to attend to regarding moving cattle. Sure enough, his ears pricked up and he demanded to know just what the problem was.

"George, you have just completed an arduous journey. You arrived here exhausted and I would be taking a big advantage of our friendship if I prevailed on you to take this drove to Carlisle."

He rose and stood over me in my chair and said, very quietly, "Bugger off, Jack. You and I go back a long way and we've been in some mighty scrapes. Carlisle is a stone's throw away from here and I can take my four dogs and a couple of young local lads who want to learn the trade and be there and back in two weeks."

There was a finality in his voice that convinced me we would come to blows, good friends as we are, if I did not allow him to help me.

Over the spring and summer months Josh Liddell my farmer had, at my insistence, bought some good quality three year old beast from the many drovers who came to our overnight stance on the long walk from Scotland to the markets of England. Using the now excellent pasture in our two hundred acre farm adjoining Ridley House, he and I had fed them on good pasture and created a very strong and healthy herd. The time had come to sell those that would do well at market and leave us with a basic herd of milking cows to provide for our needs and produce calves for the future.

This was the plan I had and after discussion with Josh, and of course George putting his two pennyworth in, we selected the cows that would travel to market.

Young men in the town, anxious to learn the droving trade but below the age of long distances, came for selection and four lucky young lads raced home to announce their imminent departure and work for money.

George told me the story:

"From an early start we made good time through Appleby, Penrith and steadily on to reach Carlisle on a market day when the cattle trade was very active. Each night we found good accommodation but in one place we kept very quiet about you because your name was still on a chalk board as 'Banned: Jack Rutherford'. The young lads worked tirelessly, ate like horses and slept well and were very little bother. In fact I think the enormity of being away from home and all the strange new sights left them somewhat in awe and they looked to me as a seasoned drover for advice and reassurance which I gave them. Some minor foolish behaviour, but we got on very well and in fact by the time we neared Carlisle they were acting instinctively and without reminders.

We had forty beast to sell and I left the boys and some of the dogs in charge of the herd and wandered in to town to get a feel for the market and prices.

Going round it became apparent that a very good trade was being done and prices were rising all morning as fewer cattle arrived but more butchers and buyers appeared. Back in the field I gathered our herd and we drove them slowly the last mile to the mart and put them all in one big holding pen. Steadily bids came, not for the whole herd but for three or four animals at a time and I established that I could ask, and get, £12.0s.0d for each animal which, as they steadily sold finally touched £12.5s.0d which was remarkable.

By 5pm we had sold all our beast, we paid our market

dues and I agreed to take the youngsters into a nearby tavern for a big hot meat pie and that news was received with great delight.

I bought them each a very weak beer and we all settled down to a very substantial meal which was well deserved.

Sitting replete in a quiet corner of the main bar, I was able, as always, to watch the comings and goings of clientele. Some rough characters came and went and I was aware that I carried over £485.0s.0d in my money belt. I had warned the youngsters to be aware of any undue attention anybody paid us.

We had arranged to stay the night in this tavern, the night drew in and the boys were looking sleepy when, to my surprise, who should walk in but Silas Kirk accompanied by the most attractive dark haired girl with beautiful dark eyes but a very woebegone look about her. Plus two great big brutes of men.

I couldn't take my eyes off her, she was the most attractive girl I had ever seen in my life and I gave her a big smile which she returned but only when Kirk and the men were not watching.

Watching her was what Kirk was doing, constantly, holding very tight to a rope around her waist and refusing to allow her a drink although he and his companions were enjoying full pints of beer.

Your comments about Kirk came back to me, Jack. Like Giselle, this girl was French, captured and offered to the highest bidder to deflower. I was livid, and with four youths to care for I should have known better, but

I walked over to the girl, smiled at her and asked for her name please.

Those eyes stared at me imploringly but any talk and conversation was stopped flat by Kirk putting his hand over her mouth and growling, "Piss off quickly because one of my men has one of your boys with a knife at his throat."

Sure enough that was the case. I very slowly drew back, watching the knife man constantly but he withdrew the knife and an uneasy truce prevailed. Suddenly the landlord appeared with four stout young men and demanded Kirk and his party leave immediately, which they did, with some bad grace. Kirk's venomous look as he left was tempered for me by the lovely smile and a small wave from the captive girl.

Jack, that brief glimpse of the girl has stayed with me ever since that moment and I am determined to find Kirk, remove him from the face of the earth, and claim that young lady for my bride."

Anyway that's how he put it when they all safely returned to Ridley House. George gave me the money and I paid off the four young men with a small bonus. They could not wait to run home to their parents and tell the tale of their travels and adventures.

I ribbed George mercilessly about his infatuation. "Where is the bloke who will never marry then?"

He remained very cool under repeated questioning and I learnt he had spoken at length to Giselle about his meeting and what the likely outcome would be for him should he meet the girl again and begin 'courting', which took me somewhat by surprise.

CHAPTER 24
RANSOM

At my request George Cook stayed with us and we tackled many of the necessary chores around the farms, rebuilding walls, and erecting fresh fencing which we had to gather from the timber merchant in town using my horse and cart. We then walked over to Bank Side Farm that I now owned to meet Josh Liddell and some of his family to whom I introduced George Cook.

Josh had diverted the stream, as we had agreed, and the pasture was now very good and was holding some nice beasts which gave us a supply of milk to the house. In fact I overheard Giselle discussing cheese making with Margaret Liddell which could be interesting.

Work needed to be done on the furthest breaches of the stream diversion which involved further trenching, laying land drains and back filling, so off with our jackets, and gathering tools, we started some long hard back breaking work trenching, laying pipes and reinstating. We didn't stop. It was stupid really but a 'man pride thing' in that Josh didn't cease, so I didn't cease. George joined in and we grafted but eventually my spade hit a large stone and bounced out of my hand so we stopped, exhausted. But on looking at our efforts we had completed a very long run of trenching.

Laughing then at our stupidity over the last three hours we wandered over to Bank Side Farm for a well earned small beer and at that point Giselle ran over the field to us in a distressed state, "Jack, Giles is missing!"

My heart stopped beating. I rose quickly and we ran together back to Ridley House, followed by George and Josh Liddell, where we were met by concerned faces and wringing hands.

Giles had been left in his baby carriage by the front gate. A great shouting had commenced in the road a distance from the house and loud banging was heard. All members of the house had congregated outside to watch and listen, leaving Giles unattended briefly and that had been the intention of the diversion I now realised. Blasted bastard Kirk had my son in his grasp.

Anger such as mine could not be appreciated and I ran far away to vent my distress on an innocent tree that I kicked and swore at, but finally responsibility returned and I joined the anxious gathering to discuss our actions.

Sitting in the kitchen at the large table I called a Council of War. Inevitably a ransom letter would be delivered shortly telling me the terms on which Kirk would deal, but I had to move very quickly to find out just what information there could be about this disaster and this was where my contacts with tinkers, packhorse men and drovers would prove invaluable because they would know just what was happening beneath the surface.

Giselle, Mary, my mother, plus Hettie were beside themselves with fear and trepidation and there was a lot of weeping and crying from those who were all so very fond of little Giles, but that must not affect my judgement. So I bade them disappear elsewhere while I plotted.

Were it me who had captured a young hostage, just what plans would I need to make, in advance, to ensure all went well?

Holding a fourteen month old child for ransom would entail a lot of forward planning. The baby would need constant attention, nursing care, baby food, constant changes of clothing and a regular sleep pattern. That was just the start. There would need to be rapid movement initially which could only mean horses then a secure hiding place that would not draw attention from nearby people with the sudden appearance of a young child.

Kirk had been seen frequently with the young girl in attendance all the time and I now guessed that her presence meant he had all along, from when I saw him in France, intended to capture Giles and the lady would attend to him. At least that is what I hoped.

Who could I rely on to help me in this quest? George Cook sat opposite me, a very stern look on his face, and I felt reassured that he was one person who would stand shoulder to shoulder with me in the conflict to come.

Kirk had at least two and probably three large bullies protecting him at all times and they would prove difficult to deal with when we went after him. I was ready to leave that very moment and go after Kirk.

George suggested, "Just calm down a little, Jack. I can imagine your thoughts right now and your wish to go off half cocked but that would be short sighted. At any moment you are expecting a ransom note and until it arrives you can only speculate on what it will contain. It will not be good news, we know that, but I think it is essential for you to stay here and comfort Giselle."

I agreed with that after some long slow angry thought but then George suggested, "I could leave immediately and start making enquiries among all your dubious friends in low places and report back to you as quickly as I can with any news."

Reuben Connor was my first thought. That scallywag would have his ear to the ground and know just what was happening in the murky underworld. I arranged for George to set off straight away to follow Reuben's tracks until he found him but under no circumstances was he to tackle Kirk. He was mine.

George set off almost immediately for places I did not dare to think about for too long. All the haunts of rogues, vagabonds, drovers, tinkers, pannier men would be carefully visited and discreet enquiries made. He's a big rough sod is George, slightly taller than me at about 6'2", broad in the shoulder, thin waist, legs like bloody tree trunks and beneath a peaceful looking exterior he is a very mean bastard in fight, no quarter given and in the same way as me, he has chosen the very rough path of a cattle drover. I just hoped he only gathered information and not skulls.

Once he was away, I concerned myself with comforting Giselle as best I could and made sure I was with her every two hours to stroke her hair, comfort her and dry her tears. She was not the only one in a distressed state, my mother and father were beside themselves with worry and doubts, as were Hetty and Jeremiah.

For two days we all moped about in a desultory fashion, attending to chores, keeping the servants busy and attending to the many people who called and offered any help and assistance they could to us which was very moving. Obviously word had spread about our dreadful situation and it was encouraging to have such strong local support from the town and far beyond in many cases.

Brooding and angry I was desperate to follow where George had gone but I had to wait at home for the inevitable ransom note that was expected at any time.

It was delivered by no less than my solicitor from Stockton-on-Tees, Dyson Frobisher who had ridden hard to make the delivery and it made me realise just how much about my life and contacts that swine Kirk knew. His contacts seemed to be endless.

With all my immediate family gathered in the kitchen, I received the letter from Dyson, slowly opened it and read out loud, "Your son Giles will be killed by me on the 15th December 1821 if you fail to pay my ransom. On that day you will have transferred to me all your property in England and France by a legal deed prepared by your so called solicitor who will deliver this message. If you attempt to trace my whereabouts or put the law onto the case the child will be slain immediately."

Gasps came from the assembled family and friends. Giselle collapsed in a faint and I rushed to her aid, laid her on a sofa and placed a cool wet cloth on her forehead in an attempt to calm her.

Mother, my father, Hetty, Jeremiah all seemed frozen in place, utterly shocked at the cruel despicable wording used by Kirk to create maximum impact. My face must have shown my rage at this attack on my family. Nobody came near me as I made sure Giselle was well cared for and then walked outside.

Dag joined me and we walked a long way together as I calmed myself down and realised that my temper and anger would affect my thinking, which was just what Kirk was relying on, for me to go off and do something stupid.

Two hours walking and thinking and I started to develop a few ideas. Kirk would need help to feed my son and change his clothes, bathe him, doubtless infrequently and that would need a woman's touch, which if I was not mistaken would be where the captured young French lady would be used.

Anywhere in the countryside a new young baby would be noticed and stand out, certainly if children's clothing and linen were being purchased. Women in the countryside immediately noticed these things and talked about them, so logic suggested a major town or city would be the most likely place for Kirk to hide. Giselle had weaned

Giles from her breasts and on to cow's milk so this major factor could be taken in to consideration when I put out my feelers for the whereabouts of the kidnappers, but the whole of England and indeed Scotland could be considered. My task grew by the moment as I considered the action I could take, but I needed George Cook back with information and quickly.

CHAPTER 25
GEORGE COOK RETURNS

Four days after leaving, a very battered, bruised and angry George Cook came back to Ridley House and his news was not good. Kirk had threatened any contacts with death if they spoke to him or me about the capture of my son and had somehow convinced some very unsavoury characters that they should thwart any investigation of mine by violence on the understanding that Kirk would soon be a very rich man and they would be paid handsomely, doubtless with my money.

George had ridden hard to Carlisle where he had last seen Kirk and his presence in the city became known to some characters who attempted to manhandle him to their long term costs, but he had to resort to using his dagger three times to remove them from his person where they had, he thought, every intention of killing him.

Despite being a marked man, he had continued his enquiries and met many of our friends from the roads who had scant information, but he learned from a tinker and his wife that a horse and cart with a man and young lady up front had been seen heading for Preston some ninety miles distant and unusually they had asked if they had any fresh milk to spare.

George had questioned them both most carefully and was convinced, from the description, that this was Kirk and the captured French girl moving south.

Now, at least, we had something to go on and I arranged for horses immediately to leave and follow the trail but as George said, "This was now seven days ago. We could be on a wild goose chase."

I had to agree that he was right but my anxiety to begin the chase was about to overtake my caution when Reuben Connor and his animals appeared, coming up the drive. Waiting for his gradual appearance I calmed down a little and put the kettle on, knowing I would be getting some good information from the man of the roads.

Greeting him with a nod outside, I invited him to join George and I at the kitchen table where I dismissed all the staff and my family so we could start talking.

Reuben said, "The word on the road is that Kirk is heading for Preston first and then may go to one of the big cities to hide from you. He is scared to death you will find him and has about eight former soldiers looking after him, checking his back trail and they all have instructions to kill you on sight. A young woman has been seen with him but no sign of a baby. They have a covered cart and a horse. The rest are either walking or on horseback, protecting the cart and allowing no travellers anywhere near. And the young lady is crying a lot."

So George's sighting had been correct but would they

stay in Preston or nearby or move on to somewhere different? I shared my opinion with Reuben that they would make for a major city to avoid curious eyes and questions and he agreed that in Kirk's place he would do just that.

How should I proceed? Reuben suggested Manchester or Liverpool could be perfect places and I was very much inclined to agree with him. The filthy back streets and downtrodden people and children would provide a perfect backdrop for him to hide in plain sight.

It was now late November. Time had flown past since the ransom note and I was ready to race over to Manchester and start enquiries but Reuben raised his hand and begged to be heard.

"Tearing over to Manchester or even Liverpool without a firm plan will waste precious time and leave you exhausted. My contacts up and down this northern part of the country are second to none, and Kirk and his bullies won't frighten the contacts I have as much as I will if they don't obey me. One word from me and many of them would be talking to the Revenue Officers for a very long time, particularly from a gaol cell. Why don't the three of us grab a decent horse each and a make a steady journey to Preston where I can make some more enquiries? But you will have to pay me for my time if it takes more than a week and I want to keep the horse."

My anger must have shown. He backed off very quickly when I rose and he suggested the latter remark was only in jest. I suggested, in strong terms, that jest was the last thing on my mind but his offer to join us was welcome. I'd seen him in a fight and he was reasonably useful.

Long conversations followed with Josh Liddell. He agreed that the care of the house, farm, drove business and all else would be in his care until Giselle became involved again.

Having made my arrangements for the care of the house and farm, I saddled up three decent horses, grabbed my money belt with its heavy buckle and we set off south at a steady pace with Dag loping along easily behind.

It was about seventy miles to Preston from Brough which we covered in three days of hard riding and sleeping at known drovers' lodgings. Word had spread that I was not a happy man. Very little was said at each stop, nods were given to me to show they knew I was deeply angry and my reputation seemed to stand me in good stead. There were no incidents until we neared Preston.

We chose a small tavern on the outskirts of the town and on reflection, as it was the obvious stopping place to intercept us if our movements were known, I found the local constable of the Watch and asked him to keep an eye on the premises and showed him my money belt with a lot of coin and paper money in it. I explained I was a drover about to buy cattle but was aware that unsavoury elements might try to rob me. He seemed delighted at the prospect of action and assured me that he and a colleague could carry out any arrests in 'their town' should anything arise.

That done to cover my actions, we took our place in the tavern and ordered some small beers. With these we chose a corner from where we could keep an eye on the entrance. Old habits die hard.

George left briefly to visit the privy outside and moments later four burly men charged into the room and literally ran at Reuben and I with hands raised and at least one a cudgel.

Dag had been to one side, slightly out of sight of these idiots. He rose and attacked in one graceful movement as I reached for my long dirk and pinned a man's hand to the wooden table before he could lift it to get to us. Screams from the man with my dog at his throat we ignored, as we did the brute attached to the table. Reuben went one way round the writhing bodies and I the other. We went straight in fast, hands, fists, boots, fingers in eyes, all the hard rough stuff we had learned in the terrible methods of drovers and tinkers over this hard land. The brutes landed some mighty punches but they had never been up against real killers and slowly we gained the upper hand, beating the standing antagonists to the ground with bleeding bits and broken limbs.

Then we turned and whilst Reuben tried to release Dag from his new friend's throat, I withdrew my dirk from the table after I had kicked the man between his legs and gained his cooperation.

Throwing him to the floor, he writhed in agony and set up a loud keening which almost matched the screams from the man whose bleeding throat Dag now viewed as a job unfinished but he had allowed Reuben to convince him to release the victim.

With a bang both the front and back doors flew open and I prepared to defend myself again although I seemed to be bleeding from somewhere.

George Cook raced in to the bar from the back door and two burly Constables of the Watch came in the front way.

All stopped and stared for it was truly a mess we had made.

George was furious and would have kicked and broken some ribs if I had not shouted a warning. Everybody in the bar just stared in amazement and kept very quiet until the landlord, seeing the Constables, confirmed that we had been viciously attacked by four men and had defended ourselves to the best of our ability. There was some disbelief in the eyes of the Law but voices around confirmed what had happened, irons appeared in the hands of the Watch, and all the brutes were bound up and formally arrested to be placed in gaol. After a few words with the Law, I was able to gather that the next Assizes would be held just after Christmas Day and I was pleased to hear that. My insistence on the Law being informed had worked very well. Four of Kirk's brutes were to be locked up safely and they were marched away in a very sorry state.

Sitting afterwards and nursing a slight cut on my arm, I noticed a distinct deference from the locals when we went for more beers, which were 'on the house' the landlord said. He had experienced a loss of trade over the past eight days whilst these men had been in his bar and they had roughed up a couple of young local lads so he was very pleased. He whispered to me, "What trade are you lads in?" and when I said we were drovers, he shook his head and whispered, "Those silly buggers didn't have a chance then. But for the Lord's sake keep that dog of yours out of sight, he's got blood all over his mouth."

This was Preston and next day we rose early to move into the town to make enquiries when I noticed we were being followed. I told the others but they had already seen the activity and thought I had gone to sleep. Cheeky buggers.

Without another word we separated and headed in different directions. It was me the man continued to follow and I knew he would meet my companions at a most inopportune moment for him but I noted another fellow had joined him and that gave me pause for thought. These men had all been employed to spy on me and probably try to kill me but thinking it through I was no good to them dead as I could not then sign any documents, relinquishing my lands, so this was a frightening effort to weaken my resolve and further they could have no idea their companions would not be available to help.

Dag stayed with me, knowing we would shortly be having fun again and it was the dog that stopped the two men from making a hasty move. I meandered into Preston centre, stopping at a road junction to allow horses and carts to go by. On looking behind, my two followers were practically on my shoulder, one carrying what looked very much like a mesh or net which they would throw over Dag but they were unaware of Reuben and George right behind them and at my signal they were both felled with heavy blows to the back of the neck. In the melee of horses and carts still passing, the lads and I took these two away by their collars and dragged them to a side street.

Brutal times call for effective action, I jumped and broke one ankle on each man and stifled their screams with their own shirts. George and Reuben were for knifing them quickly but I intended a message to be sent to any more of his gang who intended to interfere so we left them just where we dropped them although they both seemed to have broken wrists as Reuben and George dropped them back to the filthy alley.

We'd questioned them of course but they claimed they knew nothing and the threat of death wouldn't change their minds.

What did that tell me, I thought, as we considered moving silently away from the scene as their howls of pain reached a few wary onlookers. We stood with the watchers as seeming bystanders then eventually walked off with everybody else as the noise died down.

Back to the crossroads again, where we waited as more horse traffic passed and then we both saw Reuben bristle and sidle off, but not before he whispered, "Watch my back."

He was away like a streak of lightning and fit as we were it was all we could do to keep him in sight, but we did, following as best we could as he traced the route of the horses and carts and then slowed behind a very decrepit cart and a weary horse pulling a load of what seemed to be straw.

We waited and watched as Reuben waited for a quiet part of the road then he darted forward and took the horse's harness to lead it into a small almost unmade road. That action brought a shout of alarm from the covered part of the cart and a wild looking man and frighteningly large lady appeared and would have taken Reuben out if either had landed a blow to him, but we stepped in and held their arms behind them. I got a kick to my shins from the large lady, George would have had his balls pulled off but saw the move and head butted the man unconscious to the ground.

I suspected Reuben knew these two and the woman confirmed this with a use of the English language that was not really respectable, referring to Reuben's parentage and other choice phrases that gradually ceased when he brought his dagger to her throat. "Tie her up, Jack, and make sure it's good, she's a tiger in a fight."

Once accomplished, we watched as Reuben waited patiently for the man to come round. Then he again brought his knife to the man's throat this time and asked some very quiet questions to which he got some mumbled answers which he found acceptable. Rising slowly he then stirred the straw in the cart and it was immediately apparent why the horse looked so tired, it was heavy with lead which could only have come from a church roof.

Tut tutting to himself, Reuben sat in front of the man

and suggested he would like to bring the Constables over to see what was in the cart, but as a special favour to them, he would stay quiet on the matter if they would agree, on pain of death, that they had never seen any of us if asked, to which they willingly agreed.

Short wonder because stealing lead from the church roof, if found guilty, would have seen them hanged.

The three of us just walked away listening to the woman's screaming voice till we had moved far enough away for it not to bother us.

Reuben then gave us his news, the couple were the most notorious bandits in the area, well known to thieve from thieves and Reuben, bless him, had had dealings with them over the years. Neither one trusted the other and these two knew of all the skulduggery and shady goings on in the whole area. They knew where Kirk was heading as they had seen his cart and guards on the long road to Leeds which, to my mind, made sense. Massive city, stinking with the new factories and newcomers from the countryside and very few people knew their neighbours.

Retracing our steps we recovered our horses and with Dag keeping up easily we started the long journey east. As we moved George mentioned, once again, how very attractive he thought the young French lady was that Kirk was dragging around with him and idly wondered what her name might be. Reuben stared at him in wonder. "You thinking about a young lady, and a French lady at that and after all you have had to say about being single! Jack, can

I stay around a little longer and watch this please, it could be real fun."

I was glad to hear that because Reuben had proved to be a very valuable ally.

CHAPTER 26
LEEDS

By my reckoning it was about seventy five miles from Preston to Leeds along winding country roads and over some high ground. It was December now and the date of my accepting the ransom demand loomed ever closer with Kirk hidden in Leeds somewhere. My heart sank at the prospect before me and I shared my concerns with my two companions who I was leading into mortal danger.

Both looked at me in astonishment when I suggested they might want to turn back and indeed some of the language used was of a very masculine nature and largely unrepeatable. I gathered they were keen to get on with the chase so we rode hard.

I had anticipated we may need to change horses and I was reluctant to part with the three horses we had brought from home as they had proved themselves to be very strong and wiry but they were worn out. It was cold and we had to prepare ourselves.

Clitheroe was on an old drovers' road and one of the towns on our route so we diverted to buy warm clothing and gloves. I bought three very good horses at a reasonable price and arranged for our previous horses to be harnessed to follow us as spares and a change as needed. Properly dressed, we set off in what turned out to be the start of a very long winter. Snow fell, the roads clogged and our progress was frighteningly slow compared to what I wanted. Checking up, I found it was now the seventh of December, leaving me very little time and we commenced the long arduous trek from Clitheroe to Skipton then headed for Keighley and so to the outskirts of Leeds.

Despite being extremely weary from our exertions over the bleak moorland, we rode into the city which was filthy, smelly, smoky and awash with half melted snow.

Reuben knew his way around the place having had previous dealings with people here and we found ourselves in grimy back streets filled with begging urchins and people lounging about watching our every move. We looked very rich pickings to these desperate people and I resolved to rid ourselves of any excess clothing once we found a secure lodging. Reuben took us to a tavern, where an ostler took our six weary horses and we were able to secure a reasonable rent on three rooms with meals included.

George and I were left to wash and rest a little but Reuben was off out to make contact with his trading companions and though I feared for his safety I realised that to go with him in that neighbourhood would be to announce our presence to all and sundry.

Late that evening he returned with a little news. Burly

men, a girl and a baby had moved forcibly into one of the more substantial houses in the area and immediately terrorised the people in the vicinity into cowering wrecks. Men had been beaten up, ladies pestered for fresh milk and a limping figure had been seen giving orders. Could it be our man? Yes!

That evening on Reuben's return I held another Council of War with he and George. According to what he had seen, there were at least five men with Kirk plus hopefully the French girl and my son Giles. It was now a question of separating them into manageable parts, destroying each part utterly and coming away with my son intact. This was a very tall order and fraught with difficulty. Kirk's men again we suspected to be discharged soldiers who would fight a terrible battle knowing that capture would lead possibly to a death sentence. I was very reluctant to do any more killing unless it was Kirk and my thoughts ran along the lines of getting the local men of the Watch on side but Reuben went very pale at that point and suggested it was a thoroughly bad idea.

What to do? I was confident we could outwit our adversaries who were immobile and protecting a fixed location whereas we had complete flexibility of movement and could strike at will, the other side having no knowledge yet of our presence. I pondered long and hard on this and finally came up with a solution. Barges of various types moved along the Leeds Canal delivering coal, lime, cotton and manufactured goods to places as far away as London. Bargees were a very hardy crowd and would not be averse to a little kidnapping, for a suitable fee, taking any victim to a place of my choice and giving them a very rough journey into the bargain. My thoughts, when shared with George and Reuben, were considered sound and would enable us to remove at least two or three of the bastards without any word getting back to Kirk of where they had gone.

From my previous conversations with Kirk, in dreadful conditions as I recall, his constant harping on was, "Where are my men? What have you done with them?" I didn't tell him at the time but some were very dead in a bog on Stainmore, some were probably dead near a moor above Carlisle and some were now in the West Indies helping the British Navy and hopefully dying of Yellow Fever.

But it rattled him that capable men, as he thought, had failed to kill me and return so that may well have affected the quality of the people he was employing, second string men and not the brightest of intellect, possibly greedy and hungry. Could that be the way to thin them out?

Morning saw Reuben off to meet some bargemen, being some of the more unsavoury characters well known to him. By midday he returned with satisfactory results. £24.0d.0d in cash would see each person brought on board the barge being taken to Bristol eventually and it would take a long time. This bargee had a cage for live animals that was escape proof and this would suffice, he thought.

His captives would need food and water plus a pail for sanitary purposes but that was as far as he would allow.

No release until Bristol, unless they expired on the journey where the canal would swallow them up.

I could imagine no worse plight for these men than being fastened up, in a dark hold, aboard a barge, being force fed through a metal cage and living in their own crap.

Now to capture some of them. The 12th December saw me, filled with anxiety at the passage of time, hidden near the area where Kirk was holding my son Giles, and the French lady who appeared to be looking after him, together with five ruffians. My task was to spy on them, taking turns with George and Reuben, checking on any movement and establishing if there was any routine they were following. It was snowing briefly, bloody cold, but I couldn't move till it was dark. I was absolutely determined to succeed and have it out with Kirk for this terrible act of vengeance he had perpetrated against me and my family. Persevering and cursing under my breath, I watched for long hours before movement caught my eye. The French girl, tears streaming down her face, was leaving the building, carrying a loudly crying baby wrapped in cloth and escorted by two burly men. Watching with bated breath, they hurried across the street, avoiding passing horses, carts and people and practically ran to a corner shop, doubtless to collect supplies as I had suspected must happen.

Would this be repeated tomorrow? It was now noon, so I had been on watch for over four hours and hopefully George would be coming to relieve me of my vigil. I wrote on a scrap of paper roughly the time and waited for five minutes when they all hurried back, carrying parcels and beat a hasty retreat into the building, locking the door behind them.

At 2pm George appeared, silently, as if from nowhere so I gave him all the details I had, then left him on watch and went to find our tavern by a circuitous route where I warmed myself with a hot meat pie, a small beer and stood in front of a roaring fire.

Our accommodation was well away from Kirk's lair and in an area that can only be described as 'unsavoury' but the occupants of the room accepted my presence because I was dressed as scruffily as them and left me to my own devices which suited me just fine. Near the fire I gradually warmed up and waited for Reuben to reappear as he seemed to have some business to conduct with people associated with his smuggling activities. He came and sat next to me, having gathered a small beer from the serving hatch.

"It's gone very badly today," he said. "Some big bastards have muscled in on my territory, scared the wits out of my contacts and nobody will deal with me anymore. I don't like the look of things, it's getting very dangerous out there. I can feel the tension."

Listening to him whinging on, I just wondered if the same people we were interested in could also be the cause of Reuben's misery. We talked on for some time till I went to my room and lay down, exhausted by my long vigil, but at least I knew my son still lived, which gave me some hope and encouragement.

Waking swiftly from a deep sleep, I realised there was a slight change in the noise from the bar. I had slept fully dressed and I slipped quickly down and into the bar room. Reuben was pinned to his seat by two burly men, familiar to me now and they were asking him for my whereabouts. Lifting a bar stool, I cracked the first man's head open. He fell unconscious and that gave Reuben the opening he needed, out came his knife and the second man was quickly bleeding heavily from a huge cut on his right arm and he too fell to the floor.

An utter and complete silence fell in that scruffy bar, not a sound, until the moans of the assailants brought people to their feet.

"Don't you know what you've done, you fools?" someone said. "They are part of the new gang that has been terrorising this neighbourhood. We don't know where they are based but they come here and demand 'safety money' from us and we are scared stiff."

So that's where Kirk's money came from. Securing these two men took some time until the fear and terror left the remaining occupants of the room and they found some rope which we used to bind our men up.

George arrived at that moment, seriously fed up that he had missed some action, but I had him go outside and hire a handcart and a tarpaulin. This could fall right into our hands, for these were the two brutes who had accompanied the French girl and my son earlier today and I knew just where they were going and what their journey would be.

Outside with the hired handcart we bundled the groaning former soldiers on to the cart, George showing immense strength in just picking them up and throwing them bodily into the cart, ignoring their pleas for mercy. Covering the cart, we three moved through the streets of a silent wet Leeds and down to the canal where Reuben introduced the most unsavoury barge man it has been my fortune to meet, knowing he was on my side.

Below deck and in the cargo hold, we saw the large cage he had described and George once again demonstrated his prowess, lifting the men and throwing them unceremoniously into the cage and using a large padlock to retain them.

The bargee then stopped in front of me and held out his hand and at that point Reuben said, "He can't speak, but nobody ever argues with him"

Reaching into my money belt I extracted the agree £24 and I was glad to get off that bloody boat. Lord help those brutes who had helped to capture my son. If they showed any sign of resistance, they would be wiped out, I reckoned.

We returned the borrowed handcart to its owner and entered the tavern, paid our bill to date and at my insistence moved out, without a word to find another lodging but this time nearer the Kirk hideout.

Dag, I decided, would be far too obvious now to our opponents, so he was kept indoors against his will.

CHAPTER 27
M'SELLE LILLI
MARIE COLIN

Two down, three to go plus Kirk, and I was certain he would send out at least one man to find out what had happened to his cash source. Being seen in the neighbourhood of our previous tavern would be dangerous as we could not know what had happened after we left so quickly but Reuben had plenty of spies handy and one was despatched to find out the consequences of our actions. It was now the 13th December, two days from the deadline that Kirk had set and although I knew where my son was being kept, it was so secure that I was at a loss just what to do.

Waiting for the return of Reuben's spy, we held another long meeting and, depending on what we heard, we would have to concentrate on only one thing, rescuing Giles and at George's insistence, the young French lady, and all unharmed.

If we could be sure the lady and child would come out again, we could make a determined bid to overcome her bodyguards and rescue both Giles and his female helper.

Reuben knew just where we wanted to be and it was

dealt with quickly. We moved in that night and I paid up for two days. But I noticed Reuben was getting very agitated and nervous. He could now be a weak link in our venture so I took him to one side, out of George's earshot, and questioned him roughly about his attitude.

He made it quite clear. "Over many years I have built up a network of dangerous contacts in Leeds and other cities," he said, "largely because I need to buy my stolen and contraband goods at a very reasonable price to make a decent living. My whereabouts are now well known in Leeds but comment has been made that I am up to something terrible because nobody has seen my donkeys and their panniers. Word has gone round that I am working for the Customs and you two are Customs Agents."

Smiling broadly, I released his collar and let him relax once more. So that was the problem. I had thought us invisible but not to the villains on the street. Reuben's presence had set a lot of tongues wagging and he was being avoided.

There was no option, I had to let him disappear as silently as possible, recover his damned donkeys and try to resume his normal illicit life style. That very moment he shook hands with both George and I, wished us the very best of luck and I thanked him, most sincerely, for all his valuable contribution. Then he beat a hasty farewell and was gone.

Now two days only to rescue my son and hopefully the French lady before I had to capitulate and pay Kirk the

£2000 he now demanded rather than my estate. Letters had arrived from my solicitor with a revised demand and by means unknown to me Reuben had produced them that previous day.

Unknown to anybody I had that much money in paper in my money belt and despite the damned great buckle on the front I had grown used to having it next to me, but I was determined to succeed, dispose of Kirk and return intact as possible to my family.

It would be well to be armed now, with just George and I left to deal with three men plus Kirk, and they would be as familiar with swords as we were, but we hoped to have the element of surprise on our side.

By my thinking, the major weakness on their side was the constant need to attend to my son. He was receiving fresh milk daily, thank goodness. I had heard him wailing and crying for his mother which tore my heart out. Could we exploit that loophole?

Catching the villains visiting the shop again was about the only chance I could think of. If the French lady, who George thought had a lot of spirit, could be separated, with Giles, then the two bodyguards could be attacked fiercely and my son would be safe. Discussing this with George, it seemed the only feasible way of breaking the impasse before the dreadful deadline. Two days remained before I had to accept defeat and it truly rankled with me and increased my intense anger, such that George avoided me for some time until I settled down and became rational.

Our previous hiding place to spy on the house where Kirk and his men were staying was undiscovered, I believed, and it was from there we would mount any attack to rescue the hostages. I made it very clear to George that I would kill Kirk without hesitation, on sight, and accept any legal consequences. His role was, if possible, to rescue Giles and the French lady and just run away as fast as he could with them. I gave him a lot of money to cover costs and he was instructed to reach Ridley House by any means possible with them and not to look back or linger. My clear intention, once he was away, would be to flush out the remaining brutes and deal with them savagely.

With one clear day left before the deadline, we left in darkness from our tavern, having collected some bread and cheese plus a water flagon. Armed with our newly bought swords and scabbards, we made our way to the hiding place and settled down into a shift pattern to watch and wait. We had agreed one would remain on alert while the other rested, both aware we were risking our lives in this desperate attempt to save my son and my future because no way could I remain oblivious to the constant threat posed by Kirk. He had affected my life considerably and in my final judgement one of us had to die.

All bloody day we sat in that hideout, keeping quiet, watching constantly, and we were near enough to hear above the noise of horses, carts and passing people the sound of a very cross young boy wailing for his mother again. Good boy! Make a loud din, my little lad, because that means you need feeding and somebody might just venture out with you to buy fresh milk.

Two hours later and as the sky darkened to an early Winter's evening, it started to rain heavily, interspersed with hailstones. It was the cold wet conditions that George and I frequently dealt with when we were on a drove with our cattle, so we were used to it. But the lady, small child and large brute of a man who left the safety of the target house were ill prepared for the sudden change in the weather and ran with flimsy clothes over their heads and shoulders making straight for the nearby shop. Once inside, we left our hideaway, quickly stretched our aching muscles and ran with drawn swords to the shop where we stood just out of sight and waited. Out came the big brutish man first, I cut his thigh with my sword before he could react. George reversed his sword and hit him very hard with the scabbard of his weapon, as the man fell into the wet street. Oblivious.

George ran into the shop, grabbed the startled French lady and her precious bundle and had them both in his arms as he ran away, without as much as a backward glance. I raced after them and kept pace until we were well out of sight of the area when we stopped in a sheltered doorway and the most wonderful thing in my life happened right there. "Da Da," cried Giles and the French lady ceased her shaking and sobbing and looked on in amazement as my son jumped from her shoulder and into my waiting arms to be cuddled and kissed very tenderly.

Nothing wasted, George put his arms round the young lady and whispered, "You are safe now and I would like to offer my help." Smooth bloke. She fell weeping into his arms as well and I heard her say, "I just hoped and hoped you would come and rescue us." All this in a faltering French accent that sounded just fine.

Moments later, George introduced M'selle Lilli Marie Colin to me and I was deeply moved as I realised just how much care she had given my son in the most trying of circumstances. It was all very emotional.

Lilli began shaking almost uncontrollably, and explaining my plan to her took ages because she was now alone in England with no captor but without any means of support and scared out of her wits. George took charge then, the crafty bugger.

"Lilli," he said, "until you tell me otherwise I would like to be your protector and friend here in England until such time as you wish to go back to France. I will take you with me to meet Giles's mother and give you safe accommodation. Once you are over your frightening experiences, I will personally take you back to France to your parents and family."

That brought huge gasps and hundreds of tears to Lilli's face. "That swine Kirk killed my mother, knowing my father was dead and I was an only child. He wanted to sell me as a virgin bride to a man in the North of England but he has been killed." All this in a delightful hesitant English.

Clearly Kirk had followed his same lethal path as

before and seemed to be without feelings for other human beings.

Steady explanations were made and then in some haste, Lilli, my son Giles and George Cook headed off to the Stage Coach area where hopefully they would catch a fast Royal Mail Coach and escape the environs of Leeds as we had agreed. They had plenty of money for the trip and we still had a little food, although they would have to buy milk for Giles at the earliest stop, probably Wetherby.

After very long deliberation, I recovered Dag and sent him with them too. He had remained low for days. Running with the coach would do him good and I needed no distractions.

CHAPTER 28
WHERE IS KIRK?

Watching their figures disappear into the gloom of a late Winter evening and knowing they were bound, I hoped, safely for Brough and home, I stealthily retraced my steps to where we had left the seriously injured man outside the corner shop to find, to my amazement, he had gone.

Stepping carefully now I peered surreptitiously around and examined each house in turn looking for clues as to where the brute may be hiding but nothing moved. I remained where I was for a long time until the shopkeeper came out, stared round for a long time and then withdrew into his shop and reappeared with a sand bucket and a besom and promptly washed and brushed away any traces of blood that may have been on the ground before going back indoors.

Interesting, I thought. Could it be possible that the locals have decided to take matters into their own hands and gradually remove and deal with these savage strangers who had apparently been bleeding them dry with extortion?

Leaving these thoughts to one side I re-entered our

hideout and took a long hard look at the building my enemies occupied. It was a very substantial stone structure with, unusually, a stone roof and it appeared to have been erected well before any of the hovel-like brick buildings surrounding it. The very robust construction worked against me entering it, and the heavy front door, I knew from my observations, would not break down easily.

Yet three men, one of whom was my sworn enemy were within and I had to think long and hard about a way of removing and dealing with them. Dancing about in full view would encourage a rifle shot, I believed, and I could hardly knock on the door and announce I had come to kill someone! There must be a way.

Remaining vigilant, I watched the happenings on the street, urchins playing in the puddles, housewives, suitably wrapped, scurrying to the corner shop and old men strolling along the street enjoying a pipe of tobacco. All scrupulously avoided the house where Kirk and his men were hidden and I realised they had created a regime of terror in the area that would not bode then well in the event of an incident. Could I use that in my coming fight?

The more I thought about the missing brute we had felled to rescue Giles and Lilli, the more it became apparent he had been spirited away to goodness knows where by these locals who lived a hard life and would peck away at any weakness displayed by their tormentors.

Tobacco, a pipe, smoke, fire.

Looking round the derelict room we were using, I found scraps of mattress filled with straw and filthy beyond words, but dry. Also small rags and discarded scraps of a news pamphlet. In other words, enough to start a fire in the hideaway opposite and flush my victims out.

Twice in the last hours before darkness, heads had appeared at the target house door, scanning the street for the missing brute, child and carer, and their demeanour was nervous, very nervous. It seemed my tactic of picking them off one by one had succeeded in making the remaining 'troops' very nervous and prepared to stand up to Kirk and challenge his wisdom. I certainly would!

Finally after a last view down the road, the door was firmly shut and I heard the heavy lock turn in the door. Got 'em.

From their door steps there was no view of the corner shop which was literally out of sight round the corner and that created a feeling for the occupants that they had no knowledge of what had occurred nor could they question non-existent passers by.

Scrounging round behind my hideaway and out of sight of everybody, I stumbled upon a badly damaged wooded beer barrel, a rather small one identical to the huge things but smaller and manageable. Removing some dubious contents from the inside with my sword blade, I realised I had the perfect container for a very smoky fire that I could create.

Vicious sod that I am, I could not envisage setting the whole street on fire even as angry as I was, but if I could create a smoke-filled house there would be a mass exodus into my waiting sword. So I set about, filled the half barrel with straw, scraps of paper, and prepared a very effective smoke bomb. Carrying it carefully, I concealed it nearby.

Where to place the thing? Stepping warily out of my hiding place, I moved across the pavement and walked slowly in a circle until I came to the rear of the line of houses and my target clearly stood out as the only stone structure in the row. In the almost pitch dark I could make out a substantial back door so I climbed the low fence, crawled through the dense brush till I was next to the rear wall, and could identify the rear entrance in the very poor light. The hinges were on the outside which meant it opened out over only, so careful to make no noise, I created a very solid wedge out of fallen timber and a brick, and ensured the door would not open in a hurry.

Now where to place my barrel. That proved very difficult to arrange. There were no easy windows to break at the rear but looking again at the structure of the house I wondered about a cellar. If there was a cellar then there would be an entrance and if I could find it while remaining unseen and break it open, that's where my barrel would be most effective.

Figures appeared in a small window above my reach, a candle light flickered and curtains twitched. I thought I had been spotted. For what seemed a long time, a crouched figure stared through the gloom and after seven long minutes closed the curtain and the light disappeared. They were certainly on edge, but not as much as I was.

Slowly, very slowly I moved round the wall until my feet touched an obstruction and sure enough, it was an overgrown cellar entrance, hardly big enough for a small boy to wriggle through but just right for my smoke bomb.

Edging carefully back, I retraced my steps with extreme caution and made it safely back to my hideout where I collected my meagre belongings, ate the last of the bread and cheese, finished the small beer in the flagon and buckled on my sword. It would certainly be in my way as I crept through with my barrel to the cellar but I needed to be very well armed tonight. Checking my flint was working and producing a healthy spark, I set off, carrying the barrel and wishing I had George Cook's strength in my arms which I had always thought were very adequate.

It took an age for me to manoeuvre back to the cellar but time was on my side and I allowed myself the luxury of very slow movement to avoid catching the attention of any onlooker, either an enemy or a nosey local. Nothing stirred. Nearing the cellar, I checked the opening again and placed the barrel almost through the gap, leaving me enough to light my scraps of pamphlet. This would be the most dangerous part of the exercise, striking my flint and creating a big spark enough to ignite the rags and pieces of paper. So holding my coat over my head, I commenced striking, and striking, and striking until at last, with a little whoosh the flame took hold. I pushed the whole thing through the opening and heard a dull thud as it landed and smoke started billowing out of the gap which I quickly closed with the now badly wrecked door, but it contained the fumes.

Gathering my coat over my shoulders and making sure

my sword was loose in its scabbard, I ran from the rear of the building round to the front and waited. After about half an hour, shouting could be heard from within and frantic scrambling at the door with shouts of terror. At first nothing happened only the noisy shouts of "Fire" that had drawn people, who like most of us, lived in stark dread of fire and its devastating effects.

Before I could intervene, a very stout timber had been brought to the scene by six men encouraged by their wives to "Break that door down and get some water at that blaze."

That is exactly what they did.

I stood back and prepared to charge the front opening as soon as the stout timber had struck the door off its hinges. I paused, threw off my coat and went to the front of the timber battering ram to ensure I was first through that door. They counted to three and charged, hit the door a very mighty wallop and it caved in just like that!

Some fell, others tripped, but I went straight in, sword drawn and the first person I saw I swung at. He fell heavily, bleeding from his hand and as I stamped on it, I heard it break. All the time the smoke billowed about me, but I put the screaming man over my shoulder and threw him outside for the crowd to deal with.

Then I ran back in, grabbed my dropped sword and in the swirling smoke started the hunt for my quarry. Nobody else had dared to follow me into the burning building but thought I knew different. At the bottom of the stairs I found a very big brute yelling, "Help, Help," which I did by slashing his arm with my sword, then his upper leg and then dragging him out to the waiting crowd in a stream of his blood where they roughed him up and kicked him before he was tightly trussed up like a chicken, still bleeding and wailing.

Two down one, very important man to go, so I ran in again through the smoke and with drawn sword searched that whole bloody house without success. The bastard was missing!

Outside again and feeling thoroughly cheated, I was greeted with a round of applause and cheering. They thought I had rescued these brutes and saved their lives to be dealt with by the hangman. If only they knew.

Basking in this glory, I suggested it may have been just a small fire in the cellar that had been lit to keep them warm and as the smoke cleared and the wind whipped away the remains of the fumes, three of us entered the house and they searched and confirmed that some stupid bugger had tried to keep the place warm with a fire in the cellar grate. I thanked my lucky stars the barrel had rolled in that direction.

Using my newfound helpers, we searched the place from top to bottom and whilst we found plenty of evidence of a high life style on the locals' extorted money, no trace of Kirk could be found anywhere. I was about to give up in incredible anger when a young urchin pulled at my sleeve and said, "Mister, come and look at this."

That was how Kirk had escaped, three loose floorboards prised out and a hole made into the next door house where he had engineered his disappearance. Ever the resourceful murderer, desperate to save his own skin and leave his companions, foul as they were, to take the rap.

The urchin had seen a coin glistening on the floor, went to pick it up and the floor board came up and struck him on the head but he didn't let go of the coin and it was joined by another when I realised what he had found.

Kicking the floor in frustration, I left the local people recovering what they could from the debris and walked back outside. Although the crowd had thinned out a lot, a couple of big blokes, arms folded and looking very dangerous moved in my direction followed by some local ladies in shawls and bonnets. Loosening my sword again, I watched in some alarm as they hurried toward me and I took a step backwards onto the entrance to the building to give me some small advantage in what had all the appearance of a prolonged fight, the last thing I needed.

Moving towards me, the biggest man said, "Did you bring out those thieving bastards from the fire just now?"

I couldn't deny it in front of so many people and I said, "Yes, I did and they are robbing bastards but didn't deserve to die that way. What of it?"

He smiled and said, "We've been working as navvies on a new canal and just arrived home to our wives who tell us bad things about these men who we intended to deal with, but who the hell are you in all this?"

I sheathed my sword, to his relief, then suggested that the fire had made me very thirsty and I would be glad to get out of the rain to enjoy a quiet pint with him while

I explained. That's just what we all did. I bought some beers, the navvies bought some more and I explained why Jack Rutherford had made the long journey to Leeds to seek revenge for the capture and hostage of his son.

My story brought gasps of alarm and cries of shame from the people gathered near and I felt sufficiently confident in their camaraderie to ask if they had any idea of the whereabouts of the missing man from the building who I confirmed was a known murderer Silas Kirk.

Enquiries finally revealed that a man on horseback had been seen leaving the city in great haste, looking back over his shoulder but wearing a huge sword in an ornate scabbard. He was galloping east and that gave me the strange notion he would head for York and that's where I would go.

First I needed rest and a safe bed which the navvies insisted on arranging for me with the landlord and when I finally got to bed at 1am, I sank into a dreamless sleep and awoke refreshed in the knowledge that Giles was safe again and would soon be with his much relieved mother.

It was now the 16th December and York was some one and a half days' hard riding away at about twenty seven miles. I rose, enjoyed a tasty breakfast and arranged for a young boy to fetch my well rested horse and prepared for battle. Collecting some small beer in a flagon and paying for my room plus some bread and cheese, I set off to find my quarry, hoping my prediction of York was correct, because Kirk would need the anonymity of a large city and York fitted well.

CHAPTER 29
THE CHASE AND
MISS CORNELIA ELWICK

Riding my horse steadily, I enquired at each village and town, using all my contacts with drovers, bank managers, tinkers, packhorse men and scallywags of many types to find the route Kirk had taken.

Out of Leeds I asked the whereabouts of a man fleeing on horseback in Harehills, Seacroft, Whinmoor, Tadcaster, Copmanthorpe and Dringhouses. Among the contacts I had, they had seen a person in great haste on a lathered horse making for York. Perhaps I had a fixation with York but my instincts suggested it was the best place for him to run to.

Reaching York after some very hard riding, the evening of that chill 18th December found me arranging accommodation in a tavern on Micklegate and stabling my weary horse in a nearby ostlers. Worn out now and very tired, I took a hasty meal and slept heavily, waking with a late dawn.

My first stop was to see a solicitor friend with whom I had successfully conducted business. I made for his office in Stonegate, knowing he was always an early starter. Aubrey Percival was as delighted to see me again as I was him. We went straight to his office and quickly caught up on family matters and such.

Once we settled down, I told him of my quest and desire to see great harm come to my son's abductor who I had every hope was now hiding somewhere in York. Aubrey made it quite clear that under no circumstances could he become involved in my skulduggery as he had a very prominent position in the city and even our friendship could not break his vow to uphold the law.

But he used, occasionally, the services of an investigative lady who could ferret out the most minute details from her many contacts in the local underworld and she had proved remarkably efficient, particularly where fraud or deception were suspected. She unerringly identified the culprits, producing sufficient evidence to confront them, and Aubrey had achieved some remarkable results for his clients.

Aubrey hinted that the lady was very business-like, was able to charge a large fee for her services and woe betide any young man who stepped out of line in his dealings with her, particularly those of an amorous nature. A hat pin through the hand was frequently mentioned.

Also she demanded and received complete anonymity. Hers was a most unlikely form of business for a woman and she would be censured severely and shunned by ladies and men if it became known how she earned her generous living. Her perceived form of income, Aubrey said, was a very discreet ladies' hat shop.

"A ladies' hat shop? What on earth would I look like wandering in there in my scruffy travelling gear," I said in some considerable alarm but Aubrey just laughed at my discomfort and rang a little bell on his desk whereupon a clerk appeared and was given the handwritten note he waited for his employer to finish and sign. "Deliver this immediately to the Select Ladies' Hat Shop and escort Miss Elwick back here as soon as possible." Then he said, "Tea, Jack? Or would you prefer a glass of wine?" which I accepted. "We could be a few moments. Could you excuse me while I instruct my staff on the work I need completing? Make yourself comfortable."

With that, he was gone, leaving me with my thoughts of Kirk and a frosty Miss Elwick to contend with, and for the sake of my friendship with Aubrey I would engage her services but pay little heed to her advice. Bloody hat pin, he must be losing his notorious magic touch, and so it was with these angry thoughts whirling in my mind that I waited impatiently for his return and I was glad when I heard voices outside and the door opened.

Before me stood one of the most attractive, well dressed young ladies it has ever been my pleasure to meet. Rising quickly to my feet, I allowed Aubrey to make the introductions. The young lady looked most askance at me, sniffed loudly and asked Aubrey, "Are you sure about this?"

Afterwards I realised this was her way of divining my

true nature because I really let rip. "If for one moment, young lady, you think you can treat me in this most offhand way before we have hardly met you will have a nasty surprise. I will solve my immediate difficulty without your assistance and that is my final word."

Bloody woman roared with laughter, hooted and clapped her hands. "Jack, you're the man Aubrey described. I do not want a namby pamby poncy person to work for, but I do know where your Silas Kirk is hiding."

That really took the wind out of my sails. Here was a really stunning lady by all accounts, beautifully dressed with auburn hair gathered high on her head, a very smart hat in her small dainty hands and flashing blue eyes to match her blue flowing dress, all in the latest style. I would have to be extremely careful how I described Miss Cornelia Elwick to Giselle when and if we met again because I found Cornelia most attractive and I knew I may not survive my coming clash with Silas Kirk.

My hackles rose at the mention of Kirk and I looked very hard at Miss Elwick because if she was attempting to extract money from me with false information she would regret it. She immediately recognised my rising temper and asked Aubrey if we could all sit, which we did at his large desk.

"Jack Rutherford," she said, "I have had reports of your activities from my many sources and I know you are a man of great violence and determination. Your reputation is well known and I have been keeping an eye on your activities imagining that the day might come when we could meet. You should know, from what I hear, that George Cook, Lilli Colin and your son Giles are safe and nearing Ridley House where they are expected to great rejoicing. Your lovely wife Giselle is, by all accounts, coping remarkably well with your and Giles absence but is ecstatic that you have saved Giles's life. Don't even think to ask me how I know all this. I have my spies in very many places and I pay them well for information which I receive from the stage coach men and that is why my fees are so high and I get solid results. Close your mouth a little and stop gaping, this is what I do and I am brilliant at it. Do you wish to retain my services?"

For answer I closed my eyes and quietly thought, if Giselle and this one get together there will be no stopping their ambitions, but back to reality... "Yes, young lady, I am of a mind to retain you immediately and I am willing to pay some of your fee immediately, because where I am going and what I must do could end in my demise. Those are my terms."

"Accepted, I would like £400.0s.0d immediately and then we can decide on a way forward."

Reaching for my money belt round my waist, I avoided the huge buckle and removed sufficient paper money. When I handed it over, she startled me by lifting her voluminous skirt, revealing a well turned leg. She carefully placed the money in the top of her stocking, then replaced the skirt. All the while looking demurely at me and then winking broadly to an amused Aubrey.

"I think you may have met your match here, Jack," said

Aubrey with a twinkle in his eye and we then discussed at great length just what was known about Kirk. I was able to recount his murderous activities in France and his incredible dislike for me after I rescued my Giselle from his clutches. My battles on my droves with the many crooks and murderers Kirk had sent after me were mentioned as was the arrival of a new lady victim, from France, now safely in the care of a besotted George Cook. Miss Elwick or Cornelia as I was now to call her, knew most of the story apparently but was surprised when I mentioned that Cleasby had been gored to death by a bull. I mentioned my trip to France and seeing Kirk there as well.

Sitting back to review matters after Cornelia left, I now knew of Kirk's possible location but not his accomplices. She had said she would contact her spy network and bring me full details of his hiding place, his movements and any other information tomorrow morning at 10am.

My instructions, because Cornelia had taken over the planning now, were to keep a very low profile, return to my lodgings, keep out of mischief if at all possible and not draw attention to myself. Her belief was that my reputation had come to town as quickly as I had and that by all accounts Kirk was scared to death I would find and kill him. He had spies working for him too it seems.

Moving from Aubrey's office that lunchtime after a quick sandwich, I kept myself well out of notice by mingling whenever possible with any crowd going in my direction. This strategy had served me well in the

past because as I was jostled about I could scan behind.
Danger was never far.

CHAPTER 30
FIGHT TO THE DEATH

The 20th December saw me creeping nervously in the direction of the Select Ladies' Hat Shop, hoping against hope that I would not be seen by people who knew me or were sworn enemies. Why the hell they didn't have a discreet back entrance was beyond me but ladies always thought in a funny way.

Entering, I was summoned by a refined female voice to, "Shut the door, put the 'Closed Sign' up and come in here where it's warm."

I did as asked and prepared to listen.

"Here's what I know," she said. "Silas Kirk is living in a tavern on Aldwark near to the Monk's Bar part of the city wall, he has at least one man with him constantly. He acts warily and carries a huge cutlass in a decorated scabbard, which looks formidable!"

Forewarned is forearmed and I resolved to purchase a slightly lighter weapon that would be equally lethal. My twenty minutes per day sword fighting routine might now be very useful even though it bored me to death.

Leaving the shop, I walked back towards my tavern.

Glancing round for threats, it did not take me long to identify a scruffy man wearing a somewhat conspicuous black hat which he must have thought made him look tough. It identified him to me as a slow thinker and watching his movements they also appeared a little drunken, as he wobbled as he walked and followed me.

There were few bridges over the river Ouse and my accommodation on Micklegate led to the recently constructed Ouse Bridge under which the river flowed very smoothly and quickly. Could this be useful?

No, it was still broad daylight and crowds filled the street. I would have to manoeuvre him away to an alley and deal with him there but what do with the wounded man or even the carcass?

Remarkably, Black Hat solved the problem all by himself.

He waited until I was in the middle of the single carriageway Ouse Bridge and then roared loudly and charged at me, apparently very drunk, intending to knock me in the river but I saw him move and ducked down to the ground as he threw his weight at me and he went straight over the balustrade into the Ouse where he just sank.

Crowds gathered, muttering, "Drunken lout," and "Deserved it, pushing and shoving like that," and "Are you all right, Mister" to which I replied yes but a little shaken.

"It happens all the time here," someone said. "They have so much drink they think they can fly. Let's all walk quietly away and forget about it."

As a crowd we all moved off the bridge and I dodged into my lodgings and took to my room, shaking a little at yet another close escape, avoided only by my constant vigilance.

It was apparent now that Kirk knew I was in the city and had enough money to create mayhem with money for drunken sots. I needed all the help I could get.

Quickly making my way back to the Ladies' Select Hat Shop, I again let myself in and brought Cornelia up to date with the latest attempt on my life but she already had the details from her spies.

Looking at Cornelia, I realised just how attractive she was and particularly how very effective her contacts and spy network had proved to be.

"Cornelia, I will have to attack this man at the earliest possible moment and remove him, if only to reduce your fees."

A wry smile was her first reaction.

Then in great detail she described the tavern where Kirk was staying. With that vital intelligence I resolved to wait no longer and would go on the attack immediately.

She knew its clientele and was clearly giving me the message that if I went in alone I could expect an early funeral. It was a very rough place, her accomplices were unwilling to risk being maimed in a confrontation in the place and her advice was to tempt Kirk out of the inn, tackle him quickly and escape from York before there was a hue and cry over the death I contemplated.

The City Watch men had received a warning I was in

the vicinity and had orders to arrest me on sight which was a further complication.

Looking through the window in the ladies' shop, I saw it had started to snow heavily, yet another factor in my deliberations.

Decision made.

I thanked Cornelia for all her help and valuable information and left the shop to scout round and examine the layout of Kirk's tavern.

Walking in heavy snow through Deangate, I neared Aldgate and Monks Bar, keeping a wary eye on passers by and located the tavern.

A plan formed in my head. I doubled back to the dress shop and surprised Cornelia with my request that she heavily bandage my sword arm and smear it with anything that looked like blood, plus she was to put a similar 'wound' dressing on my left leg, again with the appearance of blood on it. Then, on her recommendation, I walked to a decrepit-looking shop some yards down the road, entered the place and found, to my delight, they sold swords of many types. Half an hour later I was armed with a very well balanced blade that sat in my hand as though it had lived there forever.

Using my long drover's coat, I concealed my weapon. York Watch Keepers would pounce on me instantly if they saw the blade. I wandered back to Kirk's scruffy tavern to put the next part of my plan into action.

Entering the smoky bar, I ordered a small beer and waited at the cubby hole as the beer was pulled from a nearby cask. Kirk and his crony stared in amazement at my sudden appearance and his thug would have darted at me instantly but Kirk put out a restraining hand. I could practically see him saying, "Leave this to me," because my apparent injuries had created the desired effect, that and my limp had given him the impression I was weak and vulnerable.

Easing my 'bad' leg, I limped into a corner near the door and awaited developments. Bully boy was sent to taunt and threaten me but I guessed he was only the front man before the main show.

Giving the appearance of a slightly worried man, I hastily drank my ale and went outside where the big man followed and was met outside with a sword swipe to his leg and a hard knock to his chin which left him on the ground unconscious. I had to act very quickly now and I shoved the brute around the corner, out of sight, then bent double over the ground, giving the appearance I had been wounded. Kirk practically danced out of the tavern, eyes alight with a fierce glow as he saw my apparent state of collapse.

Seeing Kirk, I rose and on faltering footsteps moved in a crawl along Aldgate, making for the Monk Bar because there, I had noticed a series of steps leading to the walls of the city and that was to be my killing area. Kirk had drawn his huge cutlass now and was following me eagerly, ready for the kill. Despite the snow some people scurried past and Kirk backed off.

Long minutes passed as I dragged my pretend poorly

leg through the gathering snow, glad to note there were no witnesses to what I hoped would happen. Careful to keep just out of reach of the swinging cutlass, I confirmed in my mind that whilst this was a killing armament it was very heavy by all its appearance and Kirk was nowhere near as robustly made as I was.

With difficult movements I finally made the steps to the city walls, facing backwards and giving the appearance of laboured steps I reached the top and my selected battlefield.

Kirk ran at me then and I only just managed to draw my sword being unable to shed my drover's coat to give me unfettered access to my sword arm. Before I could react he had taken the most mighty swipe at my stomach area. I felt the terrible blow cut across my abdomen and I waited to fall stricken before him. It hurt and Kirk backed off to watch me die, but that bloody great buckle on my money belt saved my life. To my surprise and Kirk's alarm, I rose swiftly, shed my drover's coat, released my sword and we commenced a long hard fight.

"Why can't you die like a normal man, you bastard Rutherford," Kirk shouted as he resumed his frenzied attack.

"Because you're a dead man, Kirk, and I owe you for all you have done to my family."

We fought on.

Despite the difference in age he was a skilled swordsman, I realised, and we parried blows back and forth, back and forth, my intention being to stay alive and weary him by over use of his massive cutlass. Once he slipped on the snow but despite his old leg wound, quickly recovered. I fell then, Kirk pounced and whilst I twisted away swiftly, his huge blade ripped in to my upper leg. I felt the pain immediately.

But his weapon was very heavy so avoiding a second heavy sword thrust, I rose, parried and then slid my weapon between his ribs and then withdrew it. Kirk stared aghast at the flow of blood from his side and I moved in then for the kill which I delivered with speed and fury, slicing to his throat and seeing him fall writhing to the ground where he died within seconds. I should have felt elated at his demise but truly I was exhausted and very badly hurt.

My own wound was pouring blood and I could feel myself weakening. I ripped off the false tourniquet on my arm and put a bandage on my leg to stem the flow of blood. Kirk lay sprawled on the city walls so with great effort and further bloodshed I shuffled him to the parapet and slowly manoeuvred him over the wall on to the boggy ground I had identified earlier in my preparations.

Now almost on hands and knees I needed care and attention to my injuries and a safe haven. To this day I do not know how I made that awful journey through mounting snow, marked behind with blood from my wound as I crawled and staggered till I found at last the Select Ladies' Hat Shop where the sign said 'Closed'. This I ignored and using my sword hilt knocked loudly on the door and hoped and prayed it would open. It did.

Cornelia gasped, grabbed me under the arms in a surprisingly strong way and hurried me through the shop and into the rear part that was hidden from customers. There she used a sharp knife to remove my temporary bandages and revealed the extent of my injury.

"That is a deep gash right up the front of your leg and it needs stitches immediately. I will have to leave you briefly while I find a doctor I can trust, so hold these cut parts of your leg together, don't faint and wait for my return."

For twenty long painful and terrifying minutes, I held the long gash in my upper leg as closed together as I could. The pain was excruciating and now my stomach wound made itself known.

Feeling faint and shivering in the cold room, I welcomed the sound of footsteps and the room was suddenly crowded with Cornelia, Aubrey Percival and a bewhiskered gentleman I could only assume was the doctor.

Without preamble he delved into his large leather bag, produced needle and thread and commenced sewing my wound together, giving me a very well marked piece of leather to grip my teeth into for as he said, "Some pain." It lasted fifteen long minutes but then the leg was sewn up and cleansed with alcohol which hurt most abominably. I mentioned my stomach injury.

Again, my clothes were whipped apart and a huge bruise covered the area where that mighty cutless had nearly cut me in half. All present sighed at the savage cut across the damaged belt buckle and they were all for removing it but I insisted it stayed with me, my life saver.

Given a strong dose of brandy I was placed on a temporary bed they had engineered and I slept fitfully watched over, in turn, overnight by either Cornelia or Aubrey which was very reassuring.

CHAPTER 31
BROUGH, CHRISTMAS DAY

Next morning I woke to terrible pains in my leg and an aching stomach that refused to accept the food that was offered. Aubrey asked to be excused as he needed sleep and Cornelia took over my care. My great concern now was to escape the city of York and make my way back to Brough and home.

By my calculation it was the 21st December and Christmas Day away from home again was not a prospect I wanted, but could I travel?

By drovers' roads and Royal Mail coach I could, if well, have travelled the eighty miles in two days at the most but in my present condition it would prove a nightmare.

With time on my hands, I considered just what could be done and those thoughts filled my long hours on that snowy winter day hidden in a ladies' shop in York.

My leg wound was healing nicely. No red marks or swelling but it would not bear my weight yet. I had tried it and didn't feel right. I was eating again and getting some strength back but I could not contemplate travel, even on a stretcher on a special horse and carriage. I was stuck in York with the snow continuing to fall and slow all movement outside the shop.

Cornelia's silent entry in the back room surprised me and her next remarks caused even more concern.

"Word on the street is that there is a dangerous man on the loose in the city as a man has been found badly injured outside a notorious tavern and his companion is missing. All Officers of the Town Watch are to keep an eye out and arrest a man with a very similar description to you, Jack. Much as it grieves me, I must get you out of York as quickly as possible and I would welcome any suggestions for your safety and mine."

Now this could be very handy, I thought. "Why don't you wrap me up like an old man, arrange a coach and horses which I will pay for and you could pretend you are taking a sick relative to stay with friends in the north? That way I could get out of York, and you could travel with me to say, Easingwold, from where I could be taken on to Brough. You could stay a few days in Easingwold and then come home again."

Cornelia started, "If you imagine for one moment I would let you travel out of here in your condition then you must be out of your head. It is snowing heavily and we are not even sure if the coach and horses are still running."

It went on like that for some time then she faltered to a stop and a determined look came into her eyes.

"Yes, I think that idea of yours will work. I will enquire straight away about costs and availability but by jove, Jack, it will cost you dear!"

Within the hour there was a noise outside and a large coach and horses appeared outside the rear window. It looked like a spacious vehicle with two very strong mares in the shafts. Cornelia dashed in and hustled me rather unceremoniously into some shawls and put a nightcap on my head to hide my face then two stout men came in with a stretcher. I was plonked on it and taken out straight into the carriage and stretched across two seats still on the stretcher.

Within moments we were off at a brisk pace, through Bootham Gate and north along the long road to Easingwold and beyond.

Cornelia was dressed in beautiful clothes, a fur trimming to her full length coat, smart long leather boots and a fur trimmed hat making her look most elegant.

Goodness knows what I was wearing but I hoped my boots and drover's coat had been included in this hasty retreat. Cornelia looked back somewhat longingly at her little shop as we moved down the street and she gasped and ducked down as in the distance, through the swirling snow, she glimpsed two members of the Watch nearing her shop. A very close call.

Although the coach was particularly well sprung, I still felt many of the bumps on that well rutted road out of York and the slush and snow did not help with our passage but onward we went.

Stopping for toilet breaks I was at the absolute mercy of a giggling Cornelia who had had the wit to include a wide rimmed bottle in her baggage. I do not need to tell you how we accomplished my toilet but it was more than intimate, particularly as during one piddling event the coach tipped and my member was nearly wrenched off in the bottle. My groans of discomfort were completely drowned by such girlish giggling as I have ever heard. God help me if Giselle ever heard of this.

We came to Easingwold after a slow five hour trip and stopped there for a change of horses and a brief pie and drink. Or rather Cornelia did, then she fed me and gave me the tidings. Her contacts in the coachhouse warned her she was being hunted by the Watch locally on a tip off from York the previous two hours past. There was nothing for her to do but stay with me a little longer until Thirsk where our next change of horses would occur. All this whilst snow fell intermittently and Christmas Day neared because I realised it was now late on the 21st December and an overnight stop was inevitable. Calculating, I realised Thirsk would be a poor option and that we should direct the coach to the Great North Road as soon as possible but night was closing in and accommodation was essential in my condition. Cornelia had confirmed that the two helpers sitting on top of the coach and handling the reins were employees of hers and here for the long journey which was a great comfort. But these roads were my livelihood and I had to forget the pain I was in and concentrate on a safe route for us.

Cornelia would have to stay with us so I suggested we make for Raskelf, Brafferton, Cundall, Asenby and so to the Great North Road where, with luck, a decent road surface would get us to Catterick Bridge and a stop for the night.

Frightening conditions awaited us once we left the main Thirsk to Easingwold road and only the skill of the ostlers who certainly knew their trade enabled us to at last reach the relatively easier main road. We drew into Catterick Bridge a very weary and cold group of people. The men carried me on my stretcher to the hotel where Cornelia had secured three rooms, mine, hers and a room for the men. Horses were changed, the coach was secured in the coach house, and an early start agreed for next day. We retired after a warm meal to a solid and well deserved sleep, slightly troubled on my part by the prominent role Cornelia was taking in my welfare and the possible consequences if we all turned up at Ridley House together. Sparks could fly, I thought, because these were two very strong willed ladies and my love was Giselle, without doubt.

Grey skies and fog greeted us next morning and it was with great reluctance we gathered ourselves together, left the warmth of the huge fire we had sat round over breakfast and made to coach and the main road once again. Me being stretchered in and laid across the seats which I was beginning to find ignominious.

Turning left at Scotch Corner in a mixture of rain, sleet and snow with a brisk north easterly wind blowing steadily, we made slow laborious progress to Greta Bridge and the Morritt Arms. Our journey from Catterick Bridge had spanned about fifteen miles in appalling weather and whilst I was delighted at our progress and had felt a little better over time, the state of our two coachmen beggared belief with their stout leather coats totally encrusted in driven snow. Cornelia hustled them into the warmth of the hotel, ostlers took over the horses and coach, and staff carried me in on my stretcher to the well lit interior and heat.

Today was the 23rd December, our journey times were longer than I could ever anticipate but would be further affected by the weather as we neared Stainmore, that high ground between me and home.

Although it cost me slightly more than I expected, the welcome and hospitality at the Morritt Arms was all I had heard and keeping to three rooms we all slept soundly to waken to a clear blue sky and the prospect of better travel. My instincts told me this patch of fine weather was the foretaste of another storm brewing in the north east. I was able to walk a little and had acquired a crutch to support my weight on my leg but I was not right yet and had to be most careful. At least I was relieved of the toilet arrangement and could manage myself again, thank goodness. I blushed when I thought about it.

Fed, watered, rubbed down and prancing about, our fresh horses looked keen to be off and we left in great style making for Bowes and the Unicorn Hotel. As I suspected, the fine weather stayed with us till noon, then the clouds formed, the wind rose and the going became very difficult again. It is six miles from Greta Bridge to Bowes and we were half way there when the storm hit us. The last three miles were at a walking pace. We were hardly making progress and our poor coachmen were being savaged by the elements. The storm continued and rolling down the final hill and the flat road to Bowes took the last of the strength from our poor horses who only picked up and whinnied when the stables of the Unicorn came in sight. Were we glad to reach that welcome spot!

Grooms rushed out to take the horses and secure the coach. I was just able to lower myself to the ground and avoid slipping by clutching Cornelia's shoulder then we were hustled quickly indoors to a raging fire, warm brandy and watched in alarm as steam rose in great clouds from the clothing of our hardy coachmen who quickly shed their damp garments and toasted in front of the fire.

Curious glances came my way because I am well known in these parts and it eventually came to the point where the landlord and landlady could stand it no longer.

"Jack Rutherford, you are a married man. What's going on here? We would all like to know?"

Before I could utter a word, Cornelia sprang up and raised her hand for silence. "Until we reach Ridley House and Jack's wife Giselle, I am in charge of his welfare and care after a very serious attack and wounding in Leeds City. Furthermore if any of you have any questions or problems, immediately address them to me and I will answer you. Are we all clear?"

Brilliant, just brilliant, word would spread like lightning that I was under the control of a strange lady. At least that's how I saw it at first, but as the evening wore on and we enjoyed a warm meal, the conversation always veered to Cornelia's assessment of the matter under discussion and it became evident that her role was none other than the guardian of Jack Rutherford until he could be handed to Giselle for care and nursing back to health, because I took very little part in discussions and was very early abed.

Another bright morning and this was Christmas Day. We enjoyed a sumptuous breakfast before a cheerful goodbye but this time with four horses drawing the carriage on the recommendation of both my coachmen and the landlord. From Bowes it is a very steep climb up Stainmore and in the weather we were experiencing every precaution had to be taken. I noticed our two brave coachmen had been prevailed upon to place newspapers inside their long leather coats to retain body heat for as long as possible.

Blue sky, a light breeze and the four skittish horses seemed as delighted as we were to be travelling again and with hearty Merry Christmas wishes, we left Bowes at 8.30am, after I had handsomely rewarded the whole staff for their care and attention.

Straight out of Bowes we started the long climb up Stainmore. The horses pulled steadily, the ground was now quite hard and we made good time, nearing the summit in three hours of constant travel so by about noon we felt a little confident but it was short lived. Once again the wind rose from the north east, straight into our horses' faces. They slowed and literally fought their way, encouraged by our coachmen who now walked at the horses' heads to comfort and encourage them.

We dragged the coach into Brough just as the light was fading. I showed them the direction and with my Ridley House ablaze with light we entered the drive and pulled up at the front door.

Giselle just knew. She opened the front door ran to the coach, threw the door open and fell into my arms, crying, laughing, whispering my name and causing my leg to sting but I kept quiet.

"You are home, darling. Happy Christmas. And who is this attractive lady you are with?"

Misses nothing, my girl!

Cornelia held up her hand and said, "Hello, Giselle. My name is Cornelia Elwick from York where I have been attempting to keep this young man of yours from danger and nursing him back to health and Merry Christmas."

"Merry Christmas to you too, Cornelia. Shall we go into the house? I do hope you will agree to join in our Christmas celebrations and stay with us. You gentlemen too please. You must come and get warm. Staff out here, please. Secure and feed these horses, put this coach in the coach house, bring more logs in and Jack, stop looking miserable. I love you!" All in one breath.

Giles found me then from my mother's arms and he demanded a bear hug which I returned with delight, only stopping to see a grinning George Cook, with Lilli on his arm, fluttering an engagement ring on her finger. Always a winner, that George.

Giselle delivered Cornelia into Hettie's care, and ran back, lifted my wooden crutch and gently supported me back through my own front door and to a wonderful Christmas atmosphere that had suddenly developed on my return. Linking arms, I struggled with her help and entered my dining room to be greeted by a loud cheer from the gathered throng.

That evening was spent with my family and friends in the most wonderful circumstances. We toasted frequently and I noticed Giselle and Cornelia in animated conversation which suddenly erupted in the most unladylike laughter and hand clapping, I could guess which part of the journey they had reached and I actually blushed bright red! And not even I was sure I wanted to know what business deals they were cooking up...

BIBLIOGRAPHY

Bonser. K. J. *The Drovers, who they were and how they went.*

Haldane. A.R.B. *Drove Roads of Scotland.*

Hindle. Brian Paul. *Roads and Trackways of the Lake District.*

MacDonald, Fraser George. *The Steel Bonnets.*

Roebuck, Peter. *Cattle Droving through Cumbria 1600-1900*

With kind assistance.

Werner Peene, Historian. Gistel. Belgium.

Claude and Marijke Hamilius. Gistel. Belgium.

Florent Obert. Saint Omer Tourist Information Office.

John Rowley.

Hilde Lauwers. Gistel. Belgium.

Marie Pierre Graff. Pharmacie Graff. Saint Omer.

Christine Stroobandt, Musee Portuaire Dunkerque.

The late Jeff Auty.

Vanessa Wells. Chilli Fox Design, Hampshire.

7532
608058